BOOKS BY JAMES SALTER

The Hunters
The Arm of Flesh
A Sport and a Pastime
Light Years
Solo Faces
Dusk and Other Stories

Solo Faces

A NOVEL BY

James Salter

NORTH POINT PRESS

San Francisco 1988

Originally published by Little, Brown & Co., 1979;
this edition has been revised by the author
Printed in the United States of America
Library of Congress Catalogue Card Number: 87-82585
ISBN: 0-86547-321-8

North Point Press
850 Talbot Avenue
Berkeley, California
94706

Solo Faces

I

They were at work on the roof of the church. All day from above, from a sea of light where two white crosses crowned twin domes, voices came floating down as well as occasional pieces of wood, nails, and once in the dreamlike air a coin that seemed to flash, disappear, and then shine again for an endless moment before it met the ground. Beneath the eucalyptus branches a signboard covered with glass announced the Sunday sermon: Sexuality and God.

The sun was straight overhead, pouring down on palm trees, cheap apartments, and boulevards along the sea. Sparrows hopped aimlessly between the bumpers of cars. Inland, dazzling and white, Los Angeles lay in haze.

The workmen were naked to the waist and flecked with black. One of them was wearing a handkerchief, its corners knotted, on his head. He was dipping his broom in tar and coating the shingles. He talked continuously.

"All religion begins somehow with the heat," he said. "They all started in the desert." He had the kind of youthful beard that seems like dark splinters beneath the skin. "On the other hand, if you examine it, philosophy comes from temperate regions. Intellect from the north, emotion from the south . . ."

"You're splashing that stuff, Gary."

"In California there are no ideas. On the other hand, we may see God. This is madness, working up here. I'm dying of thirst," he said. "Did you ever see *Four Feathers*? The original one—Ralph Richardson loses his helmet and the sun . . . it's like he's been hit with a sledgehammer. Bang! in five minutes he goes blind." He held out his hands for a moment, as if searching, and then lapsed into a scene from something else, "Shoot-a me! Keel-a me!" In his blackened face, teeth appeared like a sandwich unwrapped from dirty paper.

He stood and watched his companion work, steady, unhurried. The roof was shimmering, drowned in light. Far below were the doors through which women, spied on from above, had gone in and out all day. A sale was being held in the basement. On the next level, aisles and benches—he had never actually been in a church, he tried to imagine what was said there, how one behaved. Above it, he and Rand. It was all one great ascending order. Flesh, spirit, gods. Wages, three dollars an hour.

The steepness slowly reached up to him as he stood, his feet sideways on the narrow cleats. It rose in waves, he could feel it begin to enfold him. The scaffolding seemed a long way down, the ground farther. He thought of falling, not from here—he pressed with his feet, the cleats were firm—but from some unknown spire, suddenly held up by nothing, free, drifting past windows in one long instant, the shadow glimpsed incredibly from within. He stood there, staring down.

He wanted to be talked to. The work was numbing. He was bored.

"Hey, Rand."

"What?"

"I'm tired."

"Take a break," Rand said.

A breed of aimless wanderers can be found in California, working as mason's helpers, carpenters, parking cars. They somehow keep a certain dignity, they are surprisingly unashamed. It's one thing to know their faces will become lined, their plain talk stupid, that they will be crushed in the end by those who stayed in school, bought land, practiced law. Still, they have an infuriating power, that of condemned men. They can talk to anybody, they can speak the truth.

Rand was twenty-five or -six. He lived with a Mexican girl, or so they said, a tall girl whose arms were covered with fine black hair. Where had he met her, Gary wondered, what had he said to her at first? It was a summer job, Gary was merely gliding through it, he would never know. For a long time afterward, though, whenever he was in the valley and saw the dust following a lone pickup on a road through the fields, the memory would come to him, an image of a yellow Mustang, the top half-gone, the driver familiar, shirtless, wind blowing his hair.

It was a world he scorned and at the same time envied, men whose friend he would like to be, stories he would like to know.

One thing he imagined again and again was meeting ten years from now—where, he was not sure, in the northern part of the state perhaps, up in the grasslands, the bypassed towns.

He could see Rand clearly, faded, older. What he could not see was whether he had changed.

"How've you been?"

"Hi, Gary." A shrug. "Not bad. How about you? You look like you're doing all right."

"Ever get down to L.A.?"

"Oh, once in a while."

"Look me up," Gary said. "I'm just off Wilshire, here's my card . . ." And he began to describe his life, not the way he wanted to but foolishly, disliking himself as he did, talking faster, throwing one thing on top of another, like giving money to someone who stood there saying nothing, merely waiting for more. There was no way to turn from him, there must be some amount that would put gratitude in his face, that would make him murmur, thanks. Here, Gary was saying, take this and this, this, too, all of it. He was disgracing himself. He could not stop. The day was hot there in Ceres or Modesto. The rivers were stagnant, the creeks dry. Beyond the town in open meadows sheep were bleating. Rand had turned and was walking off. Despite himself, he called,

"Hey, Rand!"

What he wanted to say was, Look at me, don't you think I'm different? Can you believe I'm the same guy?

All this in the glittering light above the church, marooned like sailors on its black dorsal. He began to work again, balancing himself between the highest cleat and a gutter at the base of the dome. From there he reached up. His broom nearly touched the peak but not quite.

"You'd better put in another cleat," Rand said.

"I'm all right."

He stretched a little more. Holding the tip of the handle, balancing it, he could almost reach the top. He felt a sudden triumph. He was weightless, a lizard. He existed in a kind of airy joy. Just at that moment the world gave way—his foot slipped off the cleat. Instantly he was falling. He tried to hold on to the shingles. The broom skated down the roof. He could not even cry out.

Something hit his arm. A hand. It slid to his wrist.

"Hold on!"

He would have clutched anything, a leaf, a branch, the handle of a pail. He held tightly to Rand's hand, his feet still kicking at the air.

"Don't pull," he heard. "Don't pull, I won't be able to hold you." An inch at first and then an inch more, the pact they had managed to make was breaking. "Try not to slip!"

"I can't!" Terror was choking him.

"Get your fingers under a shingle." Rand was beginning to be pulled off himself. You could not hear it in his voice.

"I'm slipping!"

"Get hold of something."

At last he managed to. Almost by his nails he held to a shingle.

"Can you stay there?"

Gary did not answer. He was clinging to a monster by a single scale. Rand had already gone. He ran along the scaffold beneath, and hurriedly began to hammer in a cleat. A final cry came down,

"My hands are slipping!"

"It's all right. You've got a cleat. Turn face up, so you can see where you're going."

Beneath them the minister, staring upward, was holding the fallen broom.

"Is everything all right?" he called. He was a modern figure who disdained holy appearance; he drove a Porsche and mingled passages from various best-sellers with prayers for the dead. "You must have dropped this."

Gary stood on the scaffolding. He was shaking, he felt helpless.

"Thanks," was all he could say. Even later, having coffee at the food truck near the yard, he could not speak of it. He was still in a kind of daze.

"That was a close one," Rand said.

Girls from the laundry were wandering across the street in white smocks, laughing, talking. Gary felt weak, ashamed. "The scaffolding might have stopped me," he said.

"You'd have shot right past it."

"You think so?"

"Like a bird," Rand said.

2

Above Los Angeles the faint sound of traffic hung like haze. The air had a coolness, an early clarity. The wind was coming from the sea which as much as anything gives the city its aura. Morning light flooded down, onto the shops, the awnings, the leaves of every tree. It fell on lavish homes and driveways and into the faded back streets where houses with five-digit numbers languished beneath great names: Harlow Avenue, Ince Way. There are two Los Angeleses, they like to say, sometimes more, but in fact there is only one, six lanes wide with distant palms and one end vanishing in the sea. There are mythic island names of small apartments—Nalani, Kona Kai—dentists, Mexican restaurants, and women sitting on benches with undertaker's advertisements on the back. The cars shoot past like projectiles. Against the mountains tall buildings mirror the sun.

There are certain sections that are out of the way, neglected, like bits of debris in the wave. One of these is Palms. Backyards with wire fences. *For Rent* signs. Dusty screens.

Beneath a jacaranda tree shedding its leaves on the roof stood an unpainted house such as one might find in the country. There were four white posts along the porch. The yard was overgrown and filled with junk. In the back, a weedy garden. In one window, a decal of the flag. Above, an empty sky of precipitous blue. A gray cat, tail pointing straight up, was carefully making its way through the grass. Two doves clattered upward. The cat, one paw raised, watched them. In the driveway, chalky from exposure, a faded yellow car was parked.

The house belonged to a young woman from Santa Barbara. She was tall, white-skinned. It was difficult to imagine anyone describing her as Mexican. Her hair was black. Her mother was a socialite who once shot herself in the leg attempting suicide. Her father taught modern languages. Her name was Louise Rate, "R-A-T-E" she added, especially on the phone.

Rand had been living there for a year, not really in the house since his room, which he rented, was the toolshed, but he was not a tenant either. At their first interview a nervous silence fell between them, a silence during which, he later found out, she was telling herself not to speak. She opened the door to the shed and preceded him in. It was a long, narrow structure built on the back of the house. There was a bed, a dresser, shelves of old books.

"You can move these around if you like."

He gazed about. The ceiling was painted alternately white and the green of boat hulls. There were boxes of empty bottles. In the house the radio was playing; the sound came through the wall. She seemed abrupt, uninterested. That night she wrote about him in her diary.

She was a moon-child with small teeth, pale gums, awkward polished limbs. She called him by his last name. At first it seemed with scorn. It was her style.

She was working in a urologist's office. The hours suited her and also the pleasure of reading the patients' files. She was living in exile, she liked to say.

"It's sort of a mess," she had apologized. "I haven't had time to straighten it up. It's a nice street, though. It's very quiet. What sort of work do you do?"

He told her.

"I see," she said. She folded and unfolded her arms. She couldn't decide what to say. The sun was pouring down in the warm afternoon, traffic was going everywhere. Through the windows could be seen neighboring houses where the shades were always drawn as if for an illness within. And there was an illness, of lives that were spent.

"Well . . . ," she said helplessly. The stirrings of a well-being close at hand, even of a possible happiness, were confusing her. "I suppose you can have it. What's your name?"

He hardly saw her the first few days. Then, briefly appearing in the doorway, she invited him to dinner.

"It's not a party or anything," she explained.

The candles were dripping on the tablecloth. The cat walked among dishes on the sink. Louise drank wine and stole glances at him. She had never really gotten a good look at his face. He was from Indianapolis, he told her. His family had moved to California when he was twelve. He had quit college after a year.

"I didn't like the cafeteria," he said. "I couldn't stand the food or the people who ate there."

Then he had been in the army.

"The army?" she said. "What were you doing in the army?"

"I was drafted."

"Didn't you hate it?"

He didn't reply. He was sitting with his arm curved around the plate, eating slowly, like a prisoner or a man who has been in mission houses. Suddenly she understood. "Oh!" she almost said. She could see it: he was a deserter. At that moment he looked up. Don't worry, she tried to tell him silently. She admired him, she trusted him completely. He had hair that had gone too long without being cut, fine nostrils, long legs. He was filled with a kind of freedom that was almost visible. She saw where he had been. He had crossed the country, slept in barns and fields, dry riverbeds.

"I know . . . ," she said.

"Know what?"

"The army."

"You wouldn't have recognized me," he explained. "I was so gung ho, you wouldn't believe it. We had a captain, Mills was his name. He was from Arkansas, a terrific guy. He used to tell about the soldiers that gathered outside when General Marshall was dying. They stood in the dusk and sang his favorite songs. It was just the idea of it that got me. The other guys, what did they care? I wasn't like them though. I believed. I was really a soldier, I was going to officer candidate school and become a lieutenant, I was going to be the best lieutenant in the whole damned army. It was all because of that captain. Wherever he went, I wanted to go. If he died, I wanted to die."

"Is this true?"

"I used to copy the way he dressed, the way he walked. The army is like a reform school. Everyone lies, fakes. I hated that. I didn't talk to anyone, I didn't have any friends, I didn't want to be soiled. You're probably not interested in this. I don't know why I'm telling you."

"I am interested."

He paused, thinking back to a period of faith.

"We had a first sergeant, an old-timer, he could hardly write his name. We called him Bolo. I knew he liked me, I mean, I could tell. One night at a beer party I asked him about my chances for promotion. I'll never forget it. He looked at me, he kind of nodded. He said, 'Rand, I been in the army a long time, you know?' In 'knee arm forces,' is what he actually said. 'My old man was a marine, I tell you that? A China Marine. You probably never heard of the China Marines. They were the worst soldiers in the world. They had houseboys cleaned their rifles for them and shined their shoes. They had White Russian girlfriends. Why, they didn't even know how to roll a pack. I was a kid there; I remember all that. Tell you something, I was in Korea—a long time ago—that was rough. I was in Saigon. I've soldiered everywhere, you name it. I've jumped in snowstorms, we couldn't even get a squad assembled till two days later. I've jumped at night. I've jumped into rivers—by mistake, that was. I've known guys from all over, and let me tell you something: you are going to go a long way in this army, you are probably going to be one of the best soldiers there ever was."

"Did he mean it?"

"I don't know—he was drunk as a sailor."

"What happened?"

"I ran into some trouble."

The immense southern night had fallen. It glittered everywhere, in houses along the beach, supermarkets open late, the white marquees of theaters.

"Here," she said, "you want some more wine?"

"I could have been a captain."

His blue shirt was faded, his face strangely calm. He looked like a cashiered officer, like a man whose destiny has betrayed him.

"I thought you were a deserter," she confessed.

"Not in those days. I was all army." He shook his head. "*We're tenting tonight . . .* " he murmured. "I was a believer, can you imagine that?"

That night he slept in her bed. They would have been enemies otherwise. She knew she was hasty and nervous. Perhaps he wouldn't notice. The bed was very wide, her marriage bed. The sheets had scalloped edges.

"My God," she moaned. It was the first time since her divorce, she said. "Can you believe that?"

"Yeah."

"That story you told me," she said later. "Was it true?"

"What story?"

"About the marines."

He could see her there in the dark, her eyes closed.

"The marines. What marines?"

In the morning she followed him to work.

Women look like one thing when you don't know them and another when you do. It was not that he didn't like her. He would watch as she sat, dressing for the evening, before a folding mirror. In the circle of light her mysterious reflection did not even acknowledge him but watched self-absorbed as she applied the black around her eyes. Her necklaces hung from a deer antler. There were pictures cut from magazines tacked to the wall.

"Who is this?" he said. "Is this your father?"

A brief glance.

"That's D. H. Lawrence," she murmured.

A young man with a mustache and fine brown hair.

"You know who that looks like?" he said, amazed. He could hardly believe it. He turned toward her to let her guess, herself. "Hey . . . " he said, "look."

She was staring at her reflection.

"Can you believe these thin lips?" she wailed.

Yes, then he liked her. She was sardonic, pale. She wanted to be happy but could not be, it deprived her of her persona, of what would remain when he, like the rest of them, was gone. Something was always withheld, guarded, mocked. She was impatient with her son, who bore it stoically. His name was Lane, he was twelve. His room was down the hall.

"Poor Lane," she would often say, "he's not going to amount to much."

He was failing at school. The teachers liked him, he had lots of friends, but he was slow, vague, as if living in a dream.

There were nights they returned from somewhere in the city, weary from dancing, and weaved down the hallway past his door. She was making an attempt to be quiet, talking in whispers.

Her shoe dropped with the sharpness of a shot onto the floor.

"Oh, Christ," she said.

She was too tired to make love. It had been left on the dance floor. Or else she did, halfheartedly, and like two bodies from an undiscovered crime they lay, half-covered in the early light, in absolute silence except for the first, scattered sound of birds.

On Sundays they drove to the sea. In the whiteness of spring the sky was a gentle blue, a blue that has not yet felt the furnace. Small houses, lumberyards, flyblown markets. The final desolation of the coast. The streets of Los Angeles were behind them, the silver automobiles, men in expensive suits.

Seen picking their way down the slope from the highway to the beach, half-naked, towels in their hands, they seemed to be a family. As they drew closer it was even more interesting. She already had a stiffness and hesitation that are part of middle age. Her attention was entirely on her feet. Only the humorous, graceful movements of her hands and the kerchief around her head made her seem youthful. Behind her was someone tall and resigned. He hadn't yet learned that something always comes to save you.

She was a woman who would one day turn to drink or probably cocaine. She was high-strung, uncertain. She often talked about how she looked or what she would wear. She brushed the sand from her face, "What do you think of white? Pure white, the way they dress at Theodore's?"

"For what?"

"White pants with nothing underneath," she said. "White T-shirts." She was imagining herself at parties. "Just the red of lipstick and some blue around the eyes. Everything else white. Some guy comes up, some smart guy, and says, 'You know, I like the color of your nipples. You here with anyone?' I just look at him very calmly and say, 'Get lost.' "

She invented these fantasies and acted them out. One minute she would accept kisses, the next her mind would be elsewhere. And she was never really sure of him. She never dared commit herself to the idea that he would stay. Afraid of what might happen, she was frivolous, oblique, chattering to herself like a bird in a forest so as not to be aware of the approach of danger.

Early one morning he rose before five when it was barely light. The floor was cool beneath his feet. Louise was sleeping. He picked up his clothes and went down the hall. On top of rumpled sheets Lane was sleeping in his underwear. His arms were like his mother's, tubular and smooth. Rand shook him lightly. The eyes glinted open.

"You awake?" Rand asked.

There was no reply.

"Come on," he said.

3

On the parked car windows, mist had formed. Newspapers lay on the lawns. The streets were empty. Buses were driving with their lights.

The freeways were already full, a ghostly procession. Over the city lay a layer of clouds. To the east the sky was brighter, almost yellow. The bottom was spilling light. Then suddenly, breaking free from earth came the molten sun.

The buildings of downtown appeared, tall and featureless. They seemed to turn slowly and reveal an unknown face of greater detail, a planetlike face lit by the sun.

A river of cars was pouring towards them out of a brilliance that obscured the road signs. Some twenty miles farther, among the last apartment buildings and motels, were the first open hills. There was less traffic now, nurses driving homeward in their direction, Japanese, bearded blacks, their faces bathed by dawn like worshippers. It was seven o'clock.

Near Pomona the land began to open. There were orchards,

farms, vacant fields, the fields that once made up the country. A landscape more calm and pure lay all about, covered by soothing clouds. The blue breath of rain hung beneath. A group of white objects tilted like gravestones drifted by on the right.

"What are those?"

Rand glanced out at them.

"Beehives," he said.

The sky was breaking into bright fragments.

At Banning they turned off. They were far from the city now, a generation away at least. The houses were ordinary. There were trailers, limping dogs. The road had begun to climb into barren hills. At each curve was a view of wide, patterned farmland falling away below. Ahead was emptiness, land that had no owner.

"It's nice from here on," Rand said.

The mountains were the color of slate, the sun behind them. The valley, with its highway like a silver vein, was seen for the last time. Beyond it a great range of mountains had appeared, peaks still white with snow. The road was silent, smooth.

"How high are we?"

"Two, three thousand feet."

The scrub trees vanished. They were speeding through forests of pine. Along the roadside lay banks of snow.

"Look, a dog."

"That's a coyote."

It turned before they reached it and disappeared into the trees.

They dropped down into a valley and small town. Gas stations, a triangular park. It was all familiar. He knew the way as if it had been yesterday. A wooded road past houses with names like Nirvana and Last Mile, then some green water tanks, and there it was, a great dome of rock, its shoulders gleaming in the sun. A tremor of excitement went through him. The sky was clear. It was nearly nine o'clock.

They parked, the doors on both sides open, and changed their shoes. Rand got a small rucksack and coil of rope, red as flannel, from the trunk. He led the way down, off the road to a half-hidden path. They followed this for a while and then turned upward and began to climb. The pines were tall and silent. The sun trickled through them to the forest floor. Rand moved steadily, unhurriedly, almost with a hesitation between his steps. There was no point in wasting strength here. Even so, it burned the legs; sweat began to glisten on their faces. Once or twice they paused to rest.

"This is the hardest part. It's not much farther," Rand said.

"I'm okay."

A large boulder which only a glacier could have borne was up ahead, close to the base of the main rock which seemed to have lost its size. The great slabs that almost plunged into the forest had vanished. Only the lowest, nearby, could be seen.

Rand uncoiled the rope. He wrapped it twice around the boy's waist and watched as the knot was tied. The other end he tied to himself.

"You want to go first?" he said.

It was easy at the start. With the quick agility of a squirrel, Lane moved upward. After a while he heard a call,

"That's a good place to stop."

Rand began to climb. The rock felt warm, unfamiliar, not yet giving itself over. Lane was waiting in a niche forty feet above the ground.

"I'll just go on," Rand said.

Now he went first, the boy belaying. As he climbed he put in an occasional piton. He hammered them into cracks. A metal link, a carabiner, was snapped to the piton and the rope run through it.

Far below was a small upturned face. Rand climbed easily, assured in his movements. He looked, felt, then without effort, moved up.

The rock is like the surface of the sea, constant yet never the same. Two climbers going over the identical route will each manage in a different way. Their reach is not the same, their confidence, their desire. Sometimes the way narrows, the holds are few, there are no choices—the mountain is inflexible in its demands—but usually one is free to climb at will. There are principles, of course. The first concerns the rope—it is for safety but one should always climb as if the rope were not there.

"Off belay!" Rand called. He had reached a good stance, the top of an upright slab. There was a well-defined outcrop behind him. He placed a loop of nylon webbing over it and clipped to that. He pulled up what free rope there was, passing it around his waist to provide friction if necessary.

"On belay!" he called.

"Climbing," came the faint reply.

Lane had watched him carefully, but from below he could not tell much. After a few feet it was all unknown. It seemed, in places, there must have been some trick—there was no way to climb—but with the rope tugging gently at him, he managed. It was steeper than it looked. He was slight, flylike. He should have been able to cling to the merest flaws. His foot slipped off a tiny hold. He somehow caught himself. He put his toe back where it had been, with less confidence. This part was very hard. He stared up, his legs trembling. The slabs above were sheer, gleaming like the side of a ship. Beyond them, a burning blue.

He was forgetting what he should do, struggling blindly,

in desperation. His fingers ached. There was resignation heavy in his chest.

"Put your right foot where your left is!"

"What?" he cried miserably.

"Put your right foot where your left is and reach out with your left."

His fingers were losing their grip.

"I can't!"

"Try."

He did as he was told, clumsy, despairing. His foot found a hold, his hand another. Suddenly he was saved. He began to move again and in a few minutes had forgotten his fear. Reaching Rand, he grinned. He had made mistakes. He'd been leaning too close to the rock, reaching too far. His moves had not been planned. Still, he was there. A feeling of pride filled him. The ground was far below.

To the left, on a more difficult route, smooth, exposed, were two other climbers. Rand was watching them as he straightened out the rope. They were on an almost blank wall. The leader, hair pale in the sunlight, was flat against it, arms to either side, legs apart. Even in extremity he emitted a kind of power, as if he were supporting the rock. There was no one else on all of Tahquitz.

Rand turned from watching them. With a movement of his arm, he commented, "There it is."

The forest was falling beneath them, the valley. Though still far from the top, they had entered a realm of silence. There was a different kind of light, a different air.

"The next part is easier," Rand said.

The mountain had accepted them; it was prepared to reveal its secrets. The uncertainty was gone, the fear of poor holds, of places where a toe stays only because of the angle at which it is placed, indecision—one move achieves nothing, there must immediately be another, perhaps a third. Hesitate and the holds vanish, draw back.

The top was level and dusty, like the forgotten corner of a park. Sitting on a rock in the sun were the two other climbers. They were in worn shirts and climbing pants, their rope and equipment lay near their feet. The leader, who was wearing tennis shoes, glanced up as Rand approached.

"I thought that was you," Rand said. "How's it going, Jack?"

Cabot merely extended a leisurely hand. He had a broad smile and teeth with faintly jagged edges, of a lusterless white. His hair was rumpled, soiled, as if he had slept all night on a porch. He was amiable, assured. His voice had a certain warmth.

"The lost brother," he said. "Sit down. Want a sandwich?" He held one out, a graceful lack of deliberation in his movement. The sun glinted on his hair. His shoulders were strong beneath the faded shirt.

"I saw you struggling down there."

"Have you ever been on that?" Cabot asked.

"The Step?"

"You own it, right? You bastard."

"I wouldn't say that."

"Where've you been? I've been looking for you." There followed some scraps of song, Cabot singing as if to himself. "*Some say that he is sinking down to mediocrity. He even climbs with useless types like Daddy Craig and me* . . . Hey," he called to Lane who was ten feet off, not daring to join them, "how did he do? Did he manage all right?"

Rand was dividing the flattened sandwich.

"I asked everyone about you," Cabot said. "Jesus. Not a clue. You know, I thought of you so many times. Really."

He had been in Europe, in villages where the only telephone

was in a bar and the walls of the houses were two feet thick. He'd spent the summer and fall there. The names of mountains every climber knows belonged to him too now, the Cima Grande, the Blaitière, the Walker Spur.

"The Walker?"

'"Well, we didn't make it to the top," Cabot admitted. He was hunched forward a bit as if in thought. "Next time. Of course, it only comes in shape every two years, if that. You want to do it?"

"Me?"

"You've been to France, haven't you?"

"Surc. Who hasn't?" Rand said.

"You have to go. You've got to get to Chamonix. You just can't imagine. You go up the glaciers for five or six hours, you can hear the water running underneath. And what climbs!"

Rand felt his heart beating slowly, enviously. He felt unhappy, weighed down with regret. He turned to the other man,

"Did you go?" he asked.

"No," Banning said, "I'm not that lucky." He was in medical school, his climbing days were numbered.

Lane could not hear what they said, their voices were carried away by the wind. He could see them sprawled at their ease, the blond man leaning back and smiling, a piece of waxed paper fluttering near his foot. He was reminded of his mother and father talking when he had been younger, discussing things he was not meant to hear. There are conversations that mean everything, not one word of which can be imagined. He sat quietly, content to be near them, to have come this far.

Banning would become a doctor and disappear from climbing before he'd had his fill of it. Jack Cabot, it was hard to say. He was the kind of man who mapped out continents—climbing might not release him, might make him one of its myths. As for Rand, he had had a brilliant start and then defected. Something had weakened in him. That was when he was twenty, long ago. He was like an animal that has wintered somewhere, in the shadow of a hedgerow or barn, and one morning mud-stained and dazed, shakes itself and comes to life. Sitting there, he remembered past days, their glory. He remembered the thrill of height.

"Who was that?" Lane asked.

"Back there? Oh, a friend of mine."

They made their way in silence.

"Did you used to climb with him?"

Rand nodded.

"Is he good?"

"Yeah, he's good."

"He looked terrific."

"Watch your step here," Rand warned. He was moving more slowly. The slope of the rock had steepened. Towards the edge it dropped away. "I knew someone who fell here."

"Here? It's easy," Lane protested. "How could he fall?"

"He was running and he slipped."

There were boulders far below.

"That's the hard way down," Rand added.

In Chamonix the *aiguilles*, the tall pinnacles, were covered with snow. There were peaks on all sides, silent, bare. The glaciers descended slowly, half an inch an hour, centuries deep.

4

Behind the house were short sections of piñon that had lain there so long the earth had taken their shape. The wood had hardened, fragments of a column shielding a world of ants.

Swinging the hammer in heavy, rhythmic blows, Rand was splitting logs. A forgelike ringing echoed as the wedge went deep and a clear, final sound as the wood came apart. The morning surrounded him, the sun spilled down. He was shirtless. He looked like a figure in medieval battle, lost in the metal din, in glinting planes of sunshine, dust that rose like smoke.

From the house, Louise was watching with occasional glances, impatient, half-resigned, like a woman whose husband is intent on some ruinous, quixotic labor. Lane was in his room. He could hear the blows.

The car was gone, sold that morning. The sound of the wedge being driven was steady and unvarying. She went to the door.

impse of mountains. He knew no French. The clut-
s with their shops and curious signs—he did not
seriously. At the same time, he longed to know

ts of oncoming cars began to appear, a sulfur yel-
in had ceased. The mountains lay hidden in a kind
It seemed as if the stage were being set and then
t Sallanches, the valley opened. There, at its end,
, bathed in light, was the great peak of Europe,
. It was larger than one could imagine, and closer,
now. That first immense image changed his life. It
rown him, to rise with an infinite slowness like a
his head. There was nothing that could stand
nothing that could survive. Through crowded ter-
ies, rain, he had carried certain hopes and expec-
ue but thrilling. He was dozing on them like bag-
ed by the journey, and then, at a certain moment,
ad parted to reveal in brilliant light the symbol of
eart was beating in a strange, insistent way, as if
ing, as if he had committed a crime.
ived in Chamonix in the evening. The square in
station was quiet, the sky still light. He stepped
ugh mid-June, the air was chill. A taxi took two
ngers off to some hotel. He was left alone. The town
rances was empty. He had a strange impression,
rning, that he knew this place. He looked about
confirm some detail. The hotels that fronted the
ned closed; there was light in the entrance of one.
ed up to the edge of a low roof and stared at him.
e trees, were the last rays of sun. He picked up his
pack and began to walk.
s a bridge across the tracks. He went in that di-

"Hey, Rand."

His head came up.

"Don't you think you've done enough?"

"I'll be finished in a while," he said.

At last it stopped. She heard the logs being piled against the house. He came in and began to wash his hands.

"Well, I always said I'd do that. You've got enough for the winter, anyway."

"Wonderful," she commented.

"You might need it."

"I can't even make a fire," she said. He was drying his hands, brushing bits of bark from his waist. Suddenly she realized she had no way to remember this image. He was going to put on a shirt, button it. All this simply would disappear. She felt a shameful urge to reach out and embrace him, put her arms around him, fall to her knees.

They had been in a bar the night before. It was noisy, crowded. There was something he had to tell her. He was leaving, he said. She could hardly hear him.

"What?"

He repeated it. He was going away.

"When?" she asked foolishly. It was all she could manage to say.

"Tomorrow."

"Tomorrow," she said. "Going where?" She wanted to think of something incisive that would hurt him, make him stay. Instead she murmured, "You know, I really liked you."

"I'll be back."

"You mean it?"

"Sure."

"When?"

"I don't know. In a year. Maybe two."

"What are you going to do, go back to climbing? Lane told me you met your old friends."

"Friend."

"Is he going with you?"

"No."

She was looking at her glass. She suddenly turned away.

"Are you all right?"

She didn't answer.

"Louise. Come on . . ."

"Oh, forget it," she said. Her nose was running.

"I'll take you home."

"I don't want to go home."

Someone at the next table asked, "Is anything wrong?"

"Yes," she said.

"What's going on?"

"Mind your own business," Rand said.

She had already risen and was gathering her things.

They drove home in silence. She sat against the door, her narrow shoulders hunched. She was folded like an insect, legs drawn up beside her, arms crossed.

In the morning her face was swollen as if she were ill. He could hear her breathing. Somehow, it seemed conscious, sorrowful, close to a sigh. As he listened it seemed to grow louder to become, he suddenly realized, the sound of a jet crossing the city at dawn.

He left behind some cardboard boxes filled with shoes, fishing equipment, and a handful of letters from an old girlfriend, born in Kauai, who had cut his palm one night and, to seal their love, raised it to her mouth and drunk the welt of blood.

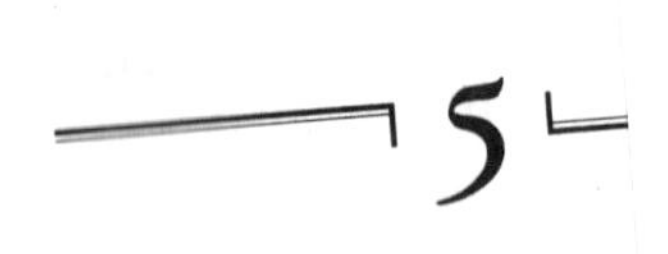

In Geneva it was raining.
There were only a few p
climbed into his seat, st
into traffic to the ceasele
the voice of a comedian
Soon they were roarin
skimming the sides of bu
permarkets sailing past.
all. They were crossing
at gardens, lumberyards
hair.
The sky went pale. A
like artillery, came the
rushed to battle, across
with mist that stretchec
The rivers were milky gr
of empty bottles stacked

clouds, a gl
tered town
take them
them.
The ligh
low. The ra
of smoke.
suddenly,
unexpecte
Mont Blan
covered in
seemed to
wave above
against it,
minals, cit
tations, va
gage, num
the clouds
it all. His
he were fle
They ar
front of th
down. Tho
other passe
to all appe
almost a w
him as if t
station see
A dog trot
Above, in t
bedroll an
There w

rection, away from town, and soon was on a dirt road. The pines had begun to darken. He came to a large villa in a garden overgrown with weeds. All sorts of junk was piled along the side, a rusted stove, flowerpots, broken chairs. Above the door was a metal sign: Chalet something-or-other, the letters had faded away. The window casements were deep, the shutters closed. He went around to the back where there was a light, and knocked.

A woman came to the door.

"Is there a place to sleep?" he asked.

She did not answer. She called into the darkness of the house and another woman, it seemed to be her mother, appeared and led him up some flights of stairs to a room where he could stay for ten francs—she made it clear by holding up two hands with outstretched fingers. There were bunks with bare mattresses. Someone's belongings were already there, shoes and equipment strewn beside the wall and on the single shelf a loaf of bread and an alarm clock.

"I'll take it," he said.

There was a washroom with one bulb. Everything was bare, unpainted, dark with years. He went to bed without dinner that night. It had begun to rain again. He heard it first, then saw it on the window. Like a beast that knows things by scent, he was untroubled, even at peace. The odor of the blankets, the trees, the earth, the odor of France seemed familiar to him. He lay there feeling not so much a physical calm as something even deeper, the throb of life itself. A decisive joy filled him, warmth and well-being. Nothing could buy these things—he was breathing quietly, the rain was falling—nothing could take their place.

6

Chamonix was at one time an unspoiled town. Though crowded and overbuilt there are aspects which remain—the narrow curving streets, the sturdy barns, the walls built thick and left to crumble—that reveal its former character and vanished appearance. It lies in a deep V in the mountains, in the valley of the Arve, a river white with rock dust that rushes in a frenzy beside the streets. Overshadowing the town are the lower slopes of Mont Blanc with the snouts of glaciers alongside.

The Alps are new mountains, forced up from the crust of the earth, folded and refolded in comparatively recent times, four or five epochs ago. Mont Blanc itself is older. It is a block mountain, formed by a vast cleaving before even the time of the dinosaurs and drowned in seas that covered Europe after they disappeared. This ancient granite rose again when the Alps were born, higher than all that now surrounded and clung to it, the highest point in Europe.

Adjoining is an army of pyramids and pinnacles, the *aiguilles*, which have drawn climbers—the English to begin with and then others—for more than a hundred years. At first sight they seem to be numberless. They lie in ranks and rough arcs to the south and east, some of the largest, like the Grandes Jorasses, almost hidden by those that are closer.

The north faces are the coldest and usually the most difficult. They receive less sun, sometimes only an hour or two a day, and are often covered in snow throughout the year. The winters are cold, the summers brief and often cloudy. The people are mountain people, hard and self-reliant—for years the Chamonix guides accepted in their ranks only those born in the valley. At the same time new roads opened the town to the world. In July and August huge crowds arrive. The restaurants, hotels, even the mountains themselves are filled. In September, as if by decree, everyone vanishes and there remains nothing but the blue letters that spell CARLTON shining mournfully at night above empty streets.

It rained for days, clouds covering the mountains, a cold steady rain. The dampness crept indoors. He sat by the stove in a plaid shirt and boots. Two young Germans who had come back soaked the first afternoon occasionally uttered a phrase or two. Bad weather, they would say. South wind is always bad. Where was he from? Ah, California! They nodded but that was all.

Then one day it was clear. The mountains appeared. There was activity everywhere, one could feel it. Chamonix with its tin roofs and small shops came forth into sunlight.

In the post office the doors to the telephone booths were constantly opening and closing, the high, impatient voices of the clerks filled the air. He stood in line. In front of him was a Japanese with a two-day growth of beard—to pay for stamps he searched in a small, canvas bag. He found a purse. He opened it. There was another, smaller purse within.

"Can you believe this?" Rand said. There was a bearded face behind him, an American face.

"Now he's going to find out he doesn't have enough money."

The Japanese had shaken some coins onto the counter; he evidently thought he had more. He shook the purse again. A single coin dropped out. Not enough.

"I'll lend it to him," Rand said. "What, do they weigh every letter?"

"Sometimes they weigh it again after you put the stamps on."

"What's the reason for that?"

"Please. It has nothing to do with reason. You've never been to France?"

His name was Neil Love. He was easy to talk to. He was a travel agent, in Chamonix for his third season. Wryly, he described the local scene which included bone-poor English stealing fruit and sitting for hours over a single bottle of beer. The Japanese were different. They came in vast numbers, armies of them, and could be found in the mountains everywhere, sleeping in cracks and upside down, frequently falling off—it was not unusual to see one in midair.

"They only buy round-trip tickets for half of them," he said. "Where are you staying?" Now was the time to get a camping site, before the crowds showed up, he advised.

"Where do you camp?"

"Come on."

He led the way. They walked up past the cemetery where Whymper, who was the first to climb the Matterhorn, lay buried. Beyond were woods. Ferns and dense greenery were everywhere. The town was not visible from here, only the sky and, opposite, the steep face of the Brévent.

"Where are we?"

"The Biolay," Love said. "Later in the year it doesn't smell too good."

He had already made up his mind about Rand judging from his clothes, the veins in his forearms, the cared-for equipment, but above all from a certain spot of coldness somewhere in him. He did not know him by reputation or name, but that meant nothing. He was absolutely sure of his sizing-up.

"What have you been climbing?" he asked.

"Nothing yet."

"You're not one of those maniacs who start out by doing the Bonatti Pillar?"

"No, I'm just getting into shape."

"It takes me all summer. Would you like to do something?"

"Whatever you like," Rand said amiably.

They decided on Pointe Lachenal. Conditions on it weren't bad, Love had heard. And the approach, in his words, was conceivable.

"What's the climb like?"

"It's rated T. D. *Très difficile*. I'm not really the world's champion climber," Love admitted.

"Is that right?"

"But I know how to climb."

What was almost a friendship sprang up between them in the green of the woods, the earth fragrant from the rain, the air pure and still. There were the blackened stones of old campfires on the ground. Love's eyeglasses glinted. "Love and Rand, that's like blood and sand . . ."

"Glove and hand."

"Much better!"

They made some tea. The pleasant hours of the afternoon passed.

Early in the morning they made their way toward the col de Rognon, a low ridge on the side of Mont Blanc. The snow was firm underfoot, not yet softened by the sun. Great peaks and pinnacles, all of them strange and unknown, were everywhere.

They were walking unroped, Love moved awkwardly. The terrain was steep.

"Good snow," Love said.

When they paused for a moment, Rand asked offhandedly, "Anyone ever show you how to self-arrest?"

"Not really," Love said.

"Let me show you. If you're falling down a slope, first you try the pick"—he demonstrated with his ice ax—"then the edge, and if neither works, drive in the shaft."

The explanation seemed to open the door to certain vague dangers. Love considered they might do well to rope up but decided to say nothing. He started off again. After a while he pointed.

"There it is."

They had crossed the ridge and off to the right, the early sun on its face, was a wall like a lump of anthracite. There were greater peaks behind but this one seemed to stand out despite its smaller size, like a menacing face in a crowd upon which one's gaze happens to fall.

At its foot Rand stared up. It was at least seven or eight hundred feet high. He reached out with his hand. The surface was chill, as if asleep. There was a vertical crack, the start of the route. He felt a sudden uncertainty as if here, for some reason, in this remote place, his ability to climb might be lost. His confidence had vanished. He put his hands on the rock, found the first foothold, and began to climb. Slowly, meter by meter, the uneasiness left him. He made his way upward.

At the first belaying stance he took off his sweater and stuffed it in his pack. The sun was warm. Love was coming up beneath, his beard already disheveled. When he raised his face he looked like a young Karl Marx.

Rand was at home. It seemed he knew instinctively where holds would be. The route was not hard to find, marked in many places by pitons which he removed as he went, clipping them into his own supply.

"We really shouldn't be taking them out," Love said. "They leave them there to save time."

"Never trust a piton you don't put in yourself."

"Isn't that a little strict?"

Rand shrugged. "On belay?"

"On belay," Love said.

"Here's a traverse. You're going to like this."

Love was beginning, psychologically, to lose ground. In places that Rand passed without comment, he found himself struggling. He knew he must climb at his own pace, but he was conscious of being slower, that someone was waiting. He flexed his fingers, his eyes on the rock in front of him, trying not to think of anything except the next hold.

The sun lay on them now with all its weight. Over Love there came a kind of dizziness, a sense of abandonment. The white of the glacier and the snowfields far below seemed to shimmer and rise. The sky was a flawless blue.

Thirty minutes later they heard something above them. Voices. They searched the face.

"Over there."

Off to the right, near a ridge toward which they were heading, were two figures. For Rand a certain pleasure he had felt was now gone; they were not alone, they were following another pair. Love listened.

"French," he said.

The leader was wearing a red sweater, talking to his second, then turning to hammer in a piton. He struck it a glancing blow—out it came. The steel rang as it hit the rock far down and shot straight out, glinting for a moment as it disappeared against the flatness of the glacier.

"*Merde.*" They were laughing and shouting at one another, their voices floating down. The leader was trying to put in another piton. It came out, too, but he caught it. Suddenly he went limp in a parody of helplessness and frustration.

Before long, they had caught up to them. Rand was fifteen feet or so below the second man. There he had to wait, interminably, unable to move. He became impatient. He looked up,

"Hello," he called.

There was a brief downward glance.

"Can we go ahead?"

They had resumed their shouts in French, they didn't answer.

Suddenly from near the leader's foot something sprang loose, gathering speed.

"Rock!" Rand hugged the wall. Leaping, arcing, the rock went by. It was the size of a shoebox. He heard it explode against the wall below.

"You son of a bitch!" he shouted. "You shouldn't be climbing! You should be playing golf!"

Love came up beside him,

"That nearly hit me," he said, concerned.

"Next time he'll kick down something bigger."

"Try and call out earlier." He leaned there resignedly, his beard awry. "My reflexes have always been a little slow. Anyway, I hope you don't mean bigger. The whole face of the Blaitière broke loose one time."

"It was probably one of these guys."

"Actually, the French are good climbers. As good as any. The Italians, too. I'm not very fond of Germans. I suppose they'd have to be included," he decided. He glanced down. They were about halfway. The glacier had become very small. It seemed he was somewhere—he had felt this many times before—where a terrible event, some suspension of physical law, might take place and everything he knew, was sure of, hoped to be, in one anarchic moment would dissolve. He saw himself falling.

This feeling alternated with one of confidence. A layer of frailty had been stripped away and a stronger, more spiritual being remained. He almost forgot where he was or what he had given himself to. His eye wandered over the silent peaks. He was awed by their immensity and stillness. He was, in a sense, part of them. Whatever happened, their majesty would enhance, even justify it. He felt equal to the climb, immeasurably close to his companion whose character he admired more and more.

"There's the aiguille du Géant," he pointed out. "And there are the Grandes Jorasses."

Rand was looking upward.

"We're going to be here all night," he said.

Finally the way was clear. The French were far ahead. Love had begun to tire, he could feel it, he was losing his strength. The rock became implacable. He could feel its malevolence.

He watched Rand above him, still in harmony with it, still

undismayed—a movement one way, no good, another slightly different, this one successful. There were times when he seemed to be doing nothing, not even exploring the surface, and then would reach out, pull, try to get his foot on some flaw. He moved in smooth advances and pauses, even retreats, like a snake swallowing a frog, motionless, then a slight flurry, then a pause. If a thing did not work he would withdraw, change position, flex his fingers to loosen them and try again. The physical acts are not hard to imagine but the endless succession of them, far up on a wall—that is another thing. And the distance beneath.

Gathering himself, Love followed. There were moments when he nearly gave up, his legs began to shake. If he fell, the rope would hold him but more than anything, more than life itself, he did not want to, he dared not fail.

Section by section, some easier, some not, they went on to the top. The others were not in sight. It was over. As they unroped, the anguish Love had felt, the shame at his weakness and lapses of will, all vanished. He knew an exultation beyond words. In his whole life, it seemed, he had never felt more worthy.

"Not a bad climb," Rand said.

"As the woman on the bus said when she saw the Pacific for the first time . . ."

"Yes?"

"I imagined it would be bigger."

They descended to the north on a slope covered with snow. It was steep, they had to stamp out steps. Suddenly Love, who had lost all thought of danger, slipped. His feet went out from under him. He began to accelerate.

"Self-arrest! Self-arrest!"

He did not make the slightest attempt to help himself but slid like a rag doll, faster, bumping, bouncing as if he would come apart. Far down, luckily, the snow was soft. He came to a stop and lay still. There were clots of ice in his beard. His knuckles were raw.

"Didn't you hear me?" Rand cried, hurrying to him.

"Oh, yes, I heard you," he said gazing up. "I heard you. I said, he is my friend."

"What?"

"My very good friend," Love said.

The public baths were in the basement of a building called La Residence, led to by a weedy path and entered through some flimsy doors. Inside was a booth where soap and towels were dispensed. It was crowded there. The doors to the showers opened and closed. There was the sound of cascading water and strange languages, the odor of steam. A woman in carpet slippers collected a franc apiece.

The woman knew Love. Where had he been climbing, she asked?

"Pointe Lachenal," he said casually.

"*Très bien*," she said. She had black hair and gold teeth. She glanced at the figure sitting next to him.

"*Avec ce monsieur?*"

Yes, Love confirmed.

"What do you suppose takes them so long?" Rand said. He was watching the shower doors.

"They're in there washing their clothes. It's forbidden, of course."

More people were coming to the entrance. Some, seeing the line, turned away. Suddenly Rand sat up.

"Hey!" he cried.

He saw the red sweater, the one that had been above them. He jumped to his feet.

"Hey, you!" He bumped into people in the doorway. "You!"

Down the corridor he ran. Near the door he grabbed the sweater. He held it tightly.

"Hey, listen. The next time," he said it slowly to have it comprehended, "I'm going to throw you right off the goddamned mountain . . ."

There was a look of utter bewilderment.

"You understand?"

A flat English voice responded, "No. Not at all. What's the trouble?"

"Weren't you climbing on Pointe Lachenal?"

As Rand released him, the Englishman straightened his clothes. He looked even smaller and more wary, like a turtle about to pull in its head.

"Sorry. There was someone on the mountain with a sweater like yours."

"So I gather," he said.

7

John Bray had, besides his red sweater, a dirty suede jacket and the face of a thief. He smoked French cigarettes. There was a fever blister on his lip. He was twenty-two.

"The guides are looking for the bastard who's pulling all their pins," he said. It was raining. They were sitting inside the National, the floor filthy from wet boots. "They don't think it's so funny."

"Too bad."

"You're screwing up their act."

"Come on. I was a guide," Rand said.

"Is that right? Where?"

"In the Tetons."

"Never heard of them. They must be new."

"Have you heard of the Himalayas?"

"The Hima-what?" Bray said. Then, in a low voice, "Look out, here they come."

A group of Japanese was entering, looking around to find an empty table.

"Hello," Bray said with a wave of his hand as they squeezed past. "Nice weather, isn't it?"

They were nodding and acknowledging the remark in some confusion.

"Having some good climbing?" he asked.

Finally they understood.

"Oh, yes. Crime," they said.

"Where have you gone? The Triolet? Grépon?"

"Yes, yes," they agreed.

"Good luck." He waved after them, smiling. "Nice little fellows," he said in an aside to Rand. "They come here by the thousands."

"I've already heard the story."

"Which one?"

"About a bit of a nip in the air."

Bray had a wry, whining laugh.

"What's that? I don't know that," he said.

Outside the rain came in gusts. The campgrounds were drenched, the paths slick with mud. The National, which was known as the English bar, was cheap and unadorned. There is a strain of English whose faces are somehow crude as if they were not worth finishing or touching with color. It was these sullen faces that filled the room.

"Never stops raining here," Bray said. "You have to wait for what they call a *beau fixe*, stretch of good weather. Then it's all right."

"Where are you going then?"

"You mean climb? I hadn't decided."

"Want to do one?"

"What are you thinking of?"

"You know the Frêney?"

Bray glanced at him. "You mean that?"

"Interested?"

"I might be, yes."

"Why not, then?"

"Um . . . be a couple of days on it, wouldn't we?"

"I would think so," Rand said. In fact he had no clear idea. The Frêney was a buttress, inaccessible and huge, on the side of Mont Blanc. There had been famous tragedies on it.

"That's where Bonatti got in all the trouble, isn't it?"

"Was it Bonatti?"

"Yeah, sure, I'd be interested," Bray said.

He had a thick cigarette in his small fingers and his head bent forward as if in suspicion. He was a plasterer. British climbing had changed since the war. Once the province of university men, it had been invaded by the working class who cut their teeth on the rock of Scotland and Wales and then traveled everywhere, suspicious and unfriendly. They came from the blackened cities of England—Manchester, Leeds. To the mountains they brought the same qualities—toughness and cynicism—that let them survive in the slums. They had no credo, no code. They had bad teeth, bad manners, and one ambition: to conquer.

8

Down a curving, dawn street in the stillness, at the hour when shutters are still closed and all that distinguishes this century from the last are empty cars ranked along the gutters, Rand walked. He was carrying a large pack and a rope. He passed almost no one—a lone woman going in the other direction and a white cat without a tail hunting in a garden. As he came close the cat stepped into some bushes. It had a tail, almost invisible, perfectly black.

At the cable car station there were people already waiting. They stood silently, some chewing bits of bread, and watched him approach. Bray had not arrived. Several guides wearing the blue enameled badge were with their clients. He slipped off his pack. Two or three stragglers came down the street. It was a few minutes before six. He felt a certain detachment. It seemed he was made of cardboard and was waiting among other cardboard figures, some of whom occasionally murmured a word or two.

There was a stirring—the ticket seller had entered the

booth inside. The crowd, like animals knowing they are about to be fed, began to press closer to the doors.

At the last moment a figure came hurrying toward him. It was one of the English climbers in a thick sweater and corduroy pants.

"John can't come," he said. "He caught some bug."

"When did that happen?"

"This morning. He has a bad throat."

The doors had been unlocked. The crowd was moving forward. It was a long walk back to camp. He had packed the night before, carefully putting everything in a certain order.

"Do you want to meet him here tomorrow?"

"No," Rand said.

"You're not going, anyway?"

"Tell him I hope it's not serious."

He was among the last to get a ticket. The cable car lurched slightly as he stepped aboard. For a moment he felt nervous, as if he had made a fatal mistake, but then they were gliding up, over the pines, ascending at a steep angle. The town began to shrink, to draw together and move off. Noiselessly they swept upward.

Bray was in a sleeping bag, his clothing scattered about. He raised himself on one elbow.

"Did you find him?" he asked.

"Yeah, he was there. I told him you were sick."

"What did he say?"

"He went up anyway."

"Went up?" Bray said.

The sun had risen. It was filling the trees with light. Bray had a moment of remorse. The day was clear, the mountains beckoned.

"He wouldn't go alone," Bray said.

"Perhaps he'll meet someone up above."

"Yeah, they're standing in line."

"Is he the one who said he'd throw you off the mountain?"

"You've got it backwards."

"You were going to throw him off?"

"No." Bray cut him short. "Did you tell him I'd go tomorrow?"

"I don't think you're going to see that much more of him."

The sky was absolutely clear and of a perfect color. It was ideal for climbing. Late in the day it became calm. The wind began to shift. Suddenly, from nowhere, there were gray streamers in the air and, as if to announce them, thunder. Climbers hurried down. Rain, which might be snow at higher altitudes, started.

The sound of it woke Bray, who had been sleeping fitfully. He was startled. He was able to see a little in the dark. It had gotten very cold. The grass of the meadow below was jerking in the rain. His thoughts, somewhat confused, went quickly to the Frêney. He imagined himself there. Like a great ship, at that moment, it was sailing through clouds and darkness. There was a sudden bolt of lightning very close. An ear-splitting clap. The silence swam back quickly and in it, like a kind of infinite debris, the snow was pouring down.

The next morning he got up early and went into town. The rescue service was in an old building next door to a garage. It was still raining. There were bicycles inside the entrance; upstairs a door slammed. Two men came down the stairs in hats and blue sweaters. They passed him and went out.

On the second floor was a bulletin board and the office. A shortwave radio was going. No one spoke English. Finally someone came to the counter who did.

"Yes?"

"I want to report someone missing."

"Where?"

"On the Frêney Pillar."

"How do you know? Were you with him?" the guide asked.

"No, he's alone," Bray said.

"Alone?" The guide was half-listening to something on the radio at which he and the others suddenly laughed. Bray waited. "Why is he alone? You know, we can't do anything until the storm has passed."

"How long is it supposed to last?" Bray demanded.

The French were always the same. They never answered a question, pretended they didn't understand. He waited until the guide, who had nothing else to do, finally noticed him again and said,

"Come back tomorrow."

"Thank you so much," he said.

They hadn't made a note, they hadn't asked for a name. He went downstairs. There were two police vans parked across the street. It was raining like winters in England, days of going to work while cars, their windows up, the interiors dry and warm, splashed past. He was used to working in the cold, in unheated houses, and going off on weekends to climb in the cold as well, not a meteor figure like Haston or Brown—it took big climbs to do that, incredible climbs—but somewhere close behind. He was lingering near the edge of things awaiting his chance. He could climb as well as any of them. The confidence on absolutely impossible routes, the spirit to dare them, that was perhaps what he lacked. It might come. In any case, he was waiting.

He walked back in the rain. The longer the storm lasted, the less were the chances. Up there it was cold, ice forming in great invincible sheets. All the features of the rock would be covered, whole routes obliterated. He was lucky, he could have been up there. Diarrhea had saved him.

"I couldn't go," he would often say later. "I was too busy."

It was one of those ironies that mark risky lives.

9

In the silence of the peaks and valleys, fading and then drifting back came the dull, unmistakable beat of rotors. From a distance the helicopter resembled an insect slanting across the snowfields, lingering, then moving on.

The rain had stopped. There was blue sky visible behind the clouds. Snow covered everything in the upper regions, every horizontal, every ledge. The summits were still shrouded, the cold clinging.

A climber was caught on the Central Pillar of Frêney, that was what they were saying. The sound of the rescue helicopter going back and forth became more and more ominous, like one of those disasters where nothing is announced but the silence tells all. Accidents were common. Occasionally there was one that stood out because of its inevitability or horror. Really cruel instances never vanished; they became part of climbing, as famous crimes become part of an era.

The search stopped in the late afternoon. A lone figure had

been seen on the glacier. At noon the next day, dirty and exhausted, the pack hanging from one shoulder, Rand came walking up the path to the campground. He looked neither to the right or left, as if there were not another soul on earth.

Love was sitting outside his tent and called to him. Rand walked on. From inside his parka he took out a bottle of wine. The cork had been pulled. Still walking, he began to drink.

On reaching the tent he simply dropped to his knees and disappeared by falling forward, his feet outside. After a moment they were drawn in behind him.

Bray found him lying there, eyes still open.

"What happened?" he asked.

Rand's gaze drifted over slowly.

"I thought they were going to bring down a frozen body," Bray said. He waited—there was no reply. Then,

"That was some *beau fixe*."

"How far up did you get? Where were you?"

Rand had closed his eyes when he lay down but only for a minute. They had opened again by themselves. He lay there teeming with words, like a dying man who could not confess, who would take them with him to the grave.

"It caught me by surprise," he finally said, "it came in so fast. I didn't have time to do anything. I got to a small ledge. At first it was just rain . . ."

"And then?"

"I stayed there. The night and the next day."

"You weren't frightened?"

"Frightened? I was paralyzed," he said. "I thought how stupid I'd been. I went up for the wrong reason, I didn't know anything. No wonder it happened."

There were other faces attempting to see in. Rand's voice, too low to be heard.

"Finally I decided I had to try and get down," he said. "I made some rappels. The rope was frozen. Hands were numb. I chopped holds. I was afraid I'd drop the ax, it would come out of my hand and that would be the end."

"Did they find you? I alerted the mountain rescue."

"They flew by. I don't know if they saw me."

Bray nodded. He was ashamed of what he had earlier felt, of having so easily given up someone for dead. The drained, low voice seemed to come from uncalculated depths, from an inner man. The weary face touched him deeply. He recognized the defeat in it, the renunciation. At that moment something bound him to Rand, he would have liked to acknowledge it but he remained silent. Instead he picked up the bottle.

"Want some?" he asked.

Rand shook his head.

"Not bad," Bray said, drinking. "Where'd you get it?"

"Don't remember."

He fell asleep. His boots were on. He was lying in the disorder of retreat, his fingernails black with dirt. He slept for eighteen hours, people walking up and down the path. In town they were already telling his story.

IO

In the fall he found a room behind the *papeterie*, along the impasse des Moulins, in a house by the river. The campground was empty, the town had become still. September light fell on everything. A lazy burning sun filled the days.

Cowbells ringing mournfully in the high meadows, the closed lives of the local people, the cool green forests—these seemed to spell out the season. The peaks were turning darker, abandoning their life. The Blaitière, the Verte, the Grandes Jorasses far up the glacier, he began to look at them another way, without eagerness or confusion. There was a different sky above them, a sky that was calm, mysterious, its color the blue of last voyages.

His hair was long, he was growing a beard—it was already fanning out, filling with wideness like a prophet from the Old Testament. They knew him in the shops where he had begun to speak a halting French. He was clean, he was dry. He walked to his room in the evening with the end of a long, narrow loaf of bread sticking out of his pack.

Later he lived in a room behind a small museum, the Musée Loppe, which was at the end of a passageway, and then in the attic of a house near the station, a large house with green shutters and faded walls. It was entered by a garden gate in the shade of an alley. Two café tables were rusting near the door. Inside was an odor of cooking and tobacco, warm, oppressive. His room had a small skylight and balcony with a set of double doors hung with curtains that once were white. Across the way was a garage and the rear of Hôtel des Étrangers. Rain fell on the metal roof. Occasionally there was the soft clatter of a train.

He stood outside Sport Giro, looking at boots in the window. Someone motioned him to come in—it was the owner at the door.

"You don't need to stand in the rain," he said.

"*Merci*."

"You speak French?"

"Not really."

"I think you do," Giro said.

The salesgirl barely glanced up. If you look like that, you don't have to speak, she remarked in French. Eventually you have to say something besides "thank you," Giro replied. Such as? she said.

Giro's homely face made an expression of resignation.

"I didn't quite understand that," Rand said.

"It's nothing."

The girl had turned away. She had a certain distance, even insolence, that annoyed him. Ordinarily he would have known how to respond but here the language baffled him.

He thought of her the next day at the baths. The water poured over him, gleaming on his limbs. Here he was more confident, unrestrained. He dreamed of possessing her, gratifying dreams. Her hands were banging on the wall, he was wading in cries . . .

The woman in her flowered wrap asked, "*Vous êtes anglais, monsieur?*"

When she found he was not, she confided in him. The English were very dirty, she said. Even the Arabs were cleaner. Had he been to England?

"England? No," he said.

Unexpectedly she smiled.

This woman at the Douches Municipales, Remy Giro, an infrequent stranger—there were not many he talked to. There was a teller at the Banque Payot who glanced at him in a certain way. She was about thirty, with a narrow face that had something hidden in it, like a woman who has ruined herself for love. He watched her boredom and absence of expression as she counted thickets of hundred-franc notes for a well-dressed businessman. When Rand stepped forward she raised her eyes for a moment. He was prepared for it. It was as if he had caught her by the arm. Sometimes he saw her from the street through the iron-barred window. She was married, he knew. He had seen the gold band on her finger.

The days grew colder, the first snows fell. It was beautiful, even seductive, with the darkness settling and snow drifting down. He felt he would journey through the winter easily, but as weeks passed he began to see how much he had been mistaken. He had ventured too far. It was like a drive across desolate country in a tiny car. The ice was on the windshield, the horizon white. If the engine failed, if he somehow happened to run off the road . . .

He had not counted on the loneliness, the terrible cold. He felt he had made a desperate error. He was stranded. The shutters of the houses were closed at night. The room was unheated, he was never really warm. Over the radio came announcements of girls who had disappeared from home—these were among the first things he was able to understand. . . . *Seize ans, mince, longeur un metre quatre-vingt, yeux verts, cheveux longs, châtains. Téléphonez* 53.36.39, etc. Sometimes he caught a few words of the news.

It was as if the battle had moved on and he had somehow been left behind in a foreign town. Everyone had gone, the camp was abandoned, he was wintering alone.

He found some illegal work—he had no permit—sweeping up in a machine shop on the road toward Geneva. It was behind the Hôtel Roma; the lighted windows and parked cars taunted him as he passed in the evening on the way home.

He thought almost every day of Louise. *Yes, come, come at once*, he wrote sitting in a bare café filling sheet after sheet of paper. He read them over slowly and sent a postcard instead. On and on came tremendous snowfalls, mountains gleaming above the town and ragged ten-franc notes received on Saturdays as pay. There was no easy way into this world.

One night on a corner he saw the teller from the bank reading the movie posters. She was alone. His heart jumped. He stood beside her.

"*Bonsoir*."

She did not answer. She turned and looked at him as if judging him coldly.

The first time she had seen him she felt herself tremble. She was susceptible to certain men, she handed her life over to them. His eyes, his burnished face—he was the type she threw everything away for, she had already done it twice.

He did not know this. He could hardly speak to her because of the language, and she seemed reluctant to talk. She had a bare, defiant face. Her husband was away somewhere visiting his parents. She had a child.

They walked by the river, the water was rattling past. He felt an almost physical pain being near her, the desire was so great. He wanted to look at her, regard her openly, see her smoke a cigarette, remove her clothes. Her name was Nicole Vix.

He managed to kiss her in a doorway. She would not tell him where she lived. She stood as if she had taken her last step on crippling heels. She put her face against his chest and allowed him to touch her breasts.

He saw her in the bank the next morning. She was not the sort of woman to smile. He didn't know how to proceed—he couldn't come in every day. Also her husband was coming back. They had exchanged a passionate signal, but as it turned out he was not able to meet her again.

The winter passed. It was difficult to remember what became of the days, they faded like those of school, the first year, the hardest. You could not tell from looking at him that he had been lonely, that he had stood at society's edge envying its light and warmth, wanting to be part of it, determined not to be; none of this was in his face.

Above, the *aiguilles* glittered. The mountains were asleep, the glaciers hidden in snow.

II

There was a single tent in the meadow. From far off it looked like the first arrival, from closer, the last survivor. Within, it had been made comfortable, some books arranged on a flat stone, an alcohol lamp, a few curled photos taped to the pole.

The grass was already knee-high, the early flowers scattered about. It was May. Huge slugs the size of fingers passed slowly across the stones. Below was the narrow road that became the path to Montenvers, although no one took it at this time of year. Above, the blue sky of France. A van had stopped on the road, tilted slightly as if in a rut.

A lone figure came up through the grass walking purposelessly, sometimes turning completely around. Rand was watching. The winter was over but he was strangely inanimate, tired of himself and the solitude that had been pressed down on him. There seemed nothing that could end it. He was lying alone among his few possessions as if wounded when suddenly he felt an overwhelming joy, like a castaway seeing a naval lieutenant in whites step onto the beach. The blond hair was shining in the sun.

"My God," he said.

"Hello, buddy." It was Cabot.

"I can't believe it. What are you doing here?"

"Looking for you."

"Stop lying. How'd you find me?"

"It wasn't hard." He looked for a place to sit. "Everybody in town seemed to know where you were."

"Yeah, I've made a lot of friends," Rand said.

"I bet you have." He looked at him closely. "So, how've you been?"

"Well, it seems to snow a lot here. A lot of people come. French mostly. Italians. I don't know who they are. Am I glad to see you. Are you here alone?"

"No. Come on down to the van."

Rand stood up. He still could not believe it. "Tell me, are you going to stay around for a while?" he said.

From the road, Carol Cabot saw them start down, her husband's arm around the other's shoulder, walking and suddenly running, not in a straight line but in great, drunken circles. She could hear shouting—it was Rand, he was making huge leaps and his arms flew about wildly. They came running up to her.

"What's happened?" she asked.

"Here he is," her husband said.

She knew Rand slightly but hardly recognized him. She tried to remember what he looked like. She had seen him only a few times and retained the image of someone tall, confident, someone with dirty hair and a kind of secret energy. Now he looked like an outlaw. He smelled of tree bark and smoke.

"Hello," she said. "When Jack said you were over here

somewhere, I thought we were going to have trouble finding you."

She was an Arizona girl, easy and optimistic, finer than her husband in certain ways. When they walked along the streets of town, she was stylish, dreaming. Her bare arms were crossed, a hand clasped on each shoulder. She would stop to look in store windows while her husband and Rand walked on and then stroll unhurriedly after them. Cabot never turned to see where she had gone. He sometimes put his arm around her, continuing to talk, when she was near. She would stay then. Often it seemed she wasn't listening.

Cabot had become stronger. He'd been working as a carpenter, framing with a heavy hammer. His forearms bulged.

"How's your French?" he asked Rand.

"Not too good."

"What? Didn't you have a French girlfriend?"

"I didn't have any kind."

Cabot suddenly admired him immensely.

"I don't believe it," Carol said calmly.

"It wasn't that I didn't give it any thought."

He seemed to them despite his appearance—as if wearing the clothes of two or three perished companions—to be particularly well. His eyes were shining. He was filled with life. They talked about it afterwards.

"He looks like some kind of holy man," Carol said.

"More like Natty Bumppo."

"Who?"

"The Deerslayer," Cabot said.

"You know I'm stupid. Who is that?"

They took him to dinner at Le Choucas—perhaps it was her face or the well-being they represented, but the heads of passersby in the street turned. The next day they drove to Saint-

Gervais and the valley beyond. Old farms with stones on the roof stood among the newer chalets. The mountains were huge and white.

"What are the conditions up there now?"

"The snow's still heavy," Rand said, "but they say it's firm. I heard them talking about it a few days ago. It isn't how much snow they have but the state it's in."

"There must be some climbs we can do. I'd like to start getting in shape."

"You look all right."

"I got very nervous being away from here. I began thinking about you, for instance. There are certain climbs I wouldn't want you to do without me."

"I think you're safe."

"Maybe for the moment, but I worry. There are climbs you just can't stop thinking about. You can't get your mind off them. Do you ever have that feeling?" He paused. "The problem is, there are other people who could do them. Keeps you awake at night."

"So, tell me, what are you thinking of?"

"We'd have to be ready."

"Come on," Rand said.

Cabot was still evasive. "We'd have to be in very good shape."

"For what?"

Cabot waited,

"The Dru," he said.

"Are you kidding? Something easy, you mean."

"Right up the middle."

A single granite face, gray and isolated, seemed to shift forward in Rand's mind, detach itself from the landscape and become even more distinct. Dark, with black lines weeping down it, a Babylonian temple smashed by centuries, its pillars and passages sheared away, the huge fragments floating through thousands of feet of air to explode on the lower slabs, legendary, unclimbable for decades: the Dru.

Rand looked at the ground. "The Dru . . ." He had a shy, almost embarrassed smile.

"What do you think?"

"Jack, I've been waiting for you," he said.

The mountain is like an immense obelisk. It was first climbed by the easiest routes. The North Face, after years of attempts, was only conquered in 1935. The West, most difficult of all, survived until after the war. It was finally climbed in 1952.

This West Face seems pointed, towering. It is like a spire. It does not reveal, from in front, its full depth and power. From the valley—Les Tines—one sees it is not a mere finger but a powerful head, the head of a god.

The regular route begins to the right, up a steep couloir that is a channel for rockfall and where a number of climbers have died. From the top of the couloir a series of terraces brings one toward the center and from there the way goes up through more than fifteen hundred feet of implacable wall.

This route was of little interest to them.

There is climbing that is tedious and requires brutal effort; it is almost a kind of destruction. To climb without holds, without natural lines, to work against the inclination of the rock, as it were, is ugly though sometimes essential. The more elegant way is rarer, like a kind of love. Here, the most hazardous attempt is made beautiful by its rightness, even if it means falling to one's death. There are weaknesses in the rock, flaws by which its smoothness can be overcome. The discovery of these and linking of them is the way to the summit.

There are routes the boldness and logic of which are overwhelming. The purely vertical is, of course, the ideal. If one could ascend, or nearly, the path that a pebble takes falling from the top and climb scarcely deviating to right or left, impossible as it may seem, one would leave behind something inextirpable, a line that led past a mere summit.

The name of that line is the direct.

In June, after three weeks of lesser climbs, they walked up to Montenvers on the steep path that wound through the forest. From here the classic outline of the Dru was visible, somewhat shadowed by the mountains behind it, distant, remote. They descended to the glacier which lay like a winter river below the station and hotel.

The glacier is dangerous only when covered with snow. That year it had melted early. The surface was gray with pulverized rock and carried granite blocks of all sizes. They passed two other people, a man and woman, both deaf—they were signing to each other as they moved in silence. From the blue of crevasses came a chill breath and the sound of trickling water. On the far side they climbed the steep bank and started along the faint track that winds up through scrub and small pines. It was warm. They walked without speaking. The Dru, visible from the glacier, had vanished behind intervening ridges. Looking up now, they saw it again, only the tip like the highest mast of a ship, then gradually the rest. They continued the long, uphill walk. It had already been three hours. The trees and undergrowth ended, there were patches of snow. At last they reached the outcrop that stood like an island in the snowfields at the foot of the Dru, the *rognon*, it was called.

It was noon. The sky was clear, the air seemed still. Above them the mythic face soared as if leaning slightly backward. The light was streaming across the top. There was snow in the great couloir, snow on the high ledges. The rock was pale in places, almost rusted. There were huge sheets like this, gilded with age. From somewhere came a faint whispering and then a roar. It was off to the right. They watched a graceful flow of rock come down the face, the snow streaming ahead of it and bursting like the sea. The sound slowly died. There was silence. The air was cold. Rand took off his pack. He stared upward.

"That is some piece of rock."

Cabot nodded. In the dank shadow it was somehow as if they had swum to this place and surfaced. The chill in the air was like spray, their faces dim.

They sat down to examine it closely. They rejected the couloir. It was off to the side as well as being the start of the normal route, but the rest was one vast apron filled with overhangs and downward-facing slabs. Almost in front of them, however, there seemed to be a slanting fault that led to a group of arches. They would come out on a sort of ledge five hundred feet up.

"Then there's a series of cracks," Cabot remarked. They were faint, vertical lines; in places they almost disappeared. It was difficult to tell if they really faded to nothing. There might be a way to link them.

Cabot was looking through binoculars—their field was small, the image unsteady and jerking. On up to an overhanging wall above which was wedged an enormous block, a well-known feature, the *bloc coincé*. Past that and up. They would be joining the end of the regular route which would take them the rest of the way.

For hours they examined it, noting every detail. Rand was writing it down with the stub of a pencil. The sun, coming over the left side, hit the face as they finished, flooding it with a vast, supernal light.

"That's about it," said Cabot finally.

Rand took the glasses for a while before they started down. He was silent. He felt a certain solemnity.

A great mountain is serious. It demands everything of a climber, absolutely all. It must be difficult and also beautiful, it must lie in the memory like the image of an unforgettable year. It must be unsoiled.

"How long do you think it's going to take?"

"Two days, maybe three," Cabot said.

"How many pitons?"

"I think everything we've got."

"Weight's going to be a problem."

Cabot didn't answer. "That's a terrific line," he said, his eye ascending one last time. "It could take us right to the top, you know?"

"Or farther."

12

He was swimming, far out to sea. Something was out there, a person, the air was ringing with faint, fading cries. His arms were heavy, the swells were becoming deeper. He tried to call out himself, his cries were borne away. Someone was drowning, he hadn't the courage to reach them. He was giving up. His heart was leaden. Suddenly he woke. He had been dreaming. It was two in the morning.

There followed hours of the same thoughts repeated again and again. The dark face of the mountain filled not only sleeplessness but the entire world. Its coldness, its hidden terrors would be revealed only at certain times. Long before dawn he lay, victim to these fears. The iron hours before the assault. His eyes were already wearied by images of what was to come, the miraculous had drained from his palms.

The weather had not been good. The delay was eating at his nerves. Each morning they woke to overcast skies or the sound of rain. Everything was ready, ropes, pitons, supplies. Every day they sat in idleness.

Weather is critical in the Alps. The sudden storms are the cause of most disasters. The casual arrival of clouds, a shifting of wind, things which might seem of little consequence can be dangerous. The sun, moreover, melts the ice and snow at higher altitudes, and rocks, sometimes of unbelievable size, break loose and fall. This happens usually in the afternoon.

One must know the mountains. Speed and judgment are essential. The classic decision is always the same, whether to retreat or go on. There comes a time when it is easier to continue upward, when the summit, in fact, is the only way out. At such a moment one must still have strength.

It cleared at last. They walked to the station. Their packs were huge, they weighed at least fifty pounds. Ropes slung over their shoulders, when they moved there was a muted clanking like the sound of armor.

His chest felt empty, his hands weightless. He felt a lack of density, the strength to cling to existence, to remain on earth, as if he were already a kind of husk that could blow away.

This great morning, this morning he would never forget. Carol was standing among the tourists. A group of schoolchildren had arrived with their teachers for an excursion to the mer de Glace. Rand stood near a post that supported the roof. The sun was warm on his legs. His clothing, different from theirs, the loaves of bread sticking out of his pack, the equipment, set him apart. A kind of distinction surrounded him, of being marked for a different life. That distinction meant everything.

They boarded the train. The seats around them were empty. Amid the shouts of children and the low, murmured talk of couples, young men with cashmere sweaters around their necks, a shrill whistle blew. The train began to move. Carol walked along beside it as far as the platform's end.

The valley fell away. On the opposite side the Brévent reared like a wall, a faint path zigzagging up it. An elderly Englishman and his wife sat nearby. He had a turned-down hat. There were blotches on his face.

"Very beautiful, isn't it?" he said.

"I prefer the Cervin. The Cervin is much nicer," his wife replied.

"Do you think so?" he said.

"It's majestic."

"Well, here you have majesty."

"Where?"

"There."

She looked for a moment.

"No," she said. "It's not the same."

The train rocked gently. The conversation seemed like scraps of paper floating from the window as they went upward. At Montenvers a crowd was waiting to go back down.

By three that afternoon they were camped beneath the Dru. That evening they had a good meal, soup, thick pieces of bread, dried fruit, tea. Afterward a bar of chocolate. They planned to start at dawn. Above them the face was silent. The slanting rays of sun fell on their shoulders, on the warm, lichened rock and dry grass. They watched the sun go down in splendor behind the shoulder of the Charmoz. Cabot was smoking. He held out the thin cigarette as he exhaled. Rand took it from between his fingers.

"Where'd you get this?"

"Brought it with me." He leaned back, his thoughts drifting off. "And so," he said, "they waited for morning. I love this time. I like it best."

"Here . . ."

Cabot reached for it. He inhaled deeply, smiled. It seemed he was a different man here, calmer; the strength remained but not the vainglory that clung to him below. The well-to-do family, school, athletic teams, what these had done for him the mountains had done for Rand. A deep companionship and understanding joined them. They were equals. Without a word, it seemed they had made a solemn pact. It would never be broken.

The light had faded. It was growing cold. By nine-thirty they were asleep. An hour later there was thunder, distant but unmistakable. By midnight it began to rain. In a torrential downpour they went down the next day, soaked and miserable. They slept in the back of the van, all three of them, piled together like dogs while chill rain beat on the roof.

Three times they were to walk to the foot of the Dru. The weather was against them. It had pinned down everyone else as well. Bray was back in town. He had talked to one of the guides, a man from the villages who knew the lore.

"There's something they call the wind for the year," he explained. "It comes on the twenty-third of January. This year it was from the west."

"What does that mean?"

"A good day, then two or three of rain, and so forth. Variable."

"I could have told you that," Cabot said.

In the second week of July they started up again. The weather had cleared, climbers were swarming into the mountains. A pair were near them on the glacier, one a girl carrying a big pack. Her boyfriend was far in front.

"What's he bringing her up for?"

"To milk her," Cabot said.

She wore glasses. Her face was damp. Later, having fallen two or three times on the ice, she cried out in frustration and sat there. The boy went on without looking back.

On the *rognon* another party was already camped—two Austrians, they looked like brothers. Cabot was immediately alarmed.

"Let's go over on the far side," he said.

That evening they could hear, from across the valley, the whistle of the last train going down. Later there was singing. It was the Austrians.

"What do you suppose they're doing? Do you think they're doing the same thing we are?"

"I don't know," Rand said. "Where were they when it was raining?"

"We'd better start early," Cabot decided.

At five in the morning they broke camp silently and went down onto the glacier that lay between them and the base of the rock. It was already light. Their hands were cold. Their footsteps seemed to bark on the frozen surface.

"If they're not up yet, this will wake them," Rand said.

"They're doing the regular route anyway."

"How do you know?"

"There they are."

There were two small figures far off on the right, making for the couloir.

"Nothing to worry about now," Rand said.

"Right."

Between the glacier and the rock there is a deep crevasse, the bergschrund; they crossed it without difficulty. The granite was dark and icy cold. Rand put his hand on it. It seemed he was touching not a face but something on the order of a planet, too vast to be imagined and at the same time, somehow, aware of his presence.

It was just before six that they began to climb.

"I'll take the first pitch, all right?" Cabot said.

He took hold of the rock, found a foothold and started up.

13

"Off belay!"

After a bit, a rope came curling down. He tied Cabot's pack to it with stiffened fingers and watched as it was hauled up, brushing against the rock. The rope came down again. He fastened his own pack to it. A few minutes later he was climbing.

At first there is anxiety, the initial twenty feet or so especially, but soon it vanishes. The rock was cold, it seemed to bite his hands. Pausing for a moment he could hear behind him the faint sound of trucks in the distant valley.

He reached the place where Cabot was belaying. They exchanged a few words. Rand went ahead. He climbed confidently, the distance beneath him deepened. The body is like a machine that is slow to start but once running smoothly can go it seems forever. He searched for holds, jamming himself in the crack, touching, rejecting, working himself higher.

By noon they were far up—they had reached a snow-covered ledge that formed the top of the apron. From here the main wall began. Rays of sun, far above, were pouring past the invisible summit. Sitting on a narrow outcrop they had something to eat.

"Not too bad, so far. Can I have some water?" Cabot said.

Somehow in taking it there was a slip—the plastic bottle dropped from his hand. He tried to catch it, but it was gone, glancing off the rock below once, twice, three times and dwindling into the white of the glacier, which after a long pause it hit.

"Sorry," he said calmly.

Rand did not comment. There was another bottle but now only half the supply remained. The mountain magnifies. The smallest event is irreversible, the slightest word.

A sequence of vertical cracks began. Rand was moving upward. At the top of the first one it was necessary to go to another off to the left. Between, it was nearly blank. The holds sloped downward. He tried, retreated, tried again. He had to reach a nub eight inches farther out. The smoothness threatened him, the lure of a last half-foot. His face was wet. His leg began to tremble. Ready, he told himself. He leaned out. Reached. His fingers touched it. He moved across. From beneath, it seemed effortless as if he were skimming the rock and barely needed holds. Cabot merely saw him put in a piton and go on. Just then the sun passed from behind the face and blinded him. He shielded his eyes. He could not be sure but he thought he saw the *bloc coincé* far above.

From Montenvers that afternoon they were visible by telescope. Large sections of the mountain were pale in the sun. Some distance beneath the great, overhanging block, two specks could be made out, motionless. A white helmet glinted.

The afternoon had passed, they were still in sunshine. The

warmth was pleasant. There is always endless waiting, looking up, neck stiff, while the leader finds the way. The silence of the face surrounded them, the greatness of the scale.

Suddenly, from nowhere, a frightening sound. The whine of a projectile; Rand hugged the wall. Something unseen came down, thudded, careened, and was gone. He looked up. Above him, an awesome sight. The brush of a great wing seemed to have passed over Cabot. As if in obedience, slowly, he was bowing. His legs went slack, his arms slipped away. Without a sound he performed a sacred act—he began to fall.

"Jack!"

The rope went taut. Cabot was hanging above him and off to one side.

"Jack! Are you all right?"

Cabot's head had fallen forward, his legs dangled. There was no reply.

One man cannot lift another with the rope, he can only hold him. Rand had a good stance but consequences were already seeping into his mind. He let some rope pass through his hands. Cabot's foot was moving slightly. It touched a hold, perhaps to use it for support, but slipped off. His head hit the wall.

"Jack! Are you okay?"

Silence.

"Jack, below you!" he called.

There was a better place farther down. Talking to him as he did, Rand eased out more rope. As a piece of clothing can catch on a sliver, something seemed to snag Cabot and he stayed, unseeing, clinging to the rock.

Rand finally worked his way up to him. At that moment Cabot's head turned slightly. His chin, the whole side of his face, was bathed in blood. His eyes were closed like someone fighting drunkenness. Blood drenched his shirt. Rand felt suddenly sick.

"How bad is it? Let me see."

He half-expected the wet gleam of brains as he removed the helmet. The blood rushed forth. It was dripping from the jaw.

"Do you have a bandage?"

"No," Cabot barely muttered.

He made one with a handkerchief that darkened as he tied it. He wiped the jaw to see if the flow was stopping. His heart pounded. He tried to see if blood was coming from the ear, which meant serious concussion or a fractured skull.

One thing seemed certain even at that moment: Cabot was going to die.

"Does it hurt?"

A slow nod. The blood would not stop. Rand wiped his fingers on the rock and tried to collect fleeing thoughts. He hammered in a piton and clipped them both to it. Cabot's head dropped forward as if he were asleep. A thousand feet lay below them. There were two or three hours of daylight left. In any case they could not stay here.

Some distance above was an overhang that might conceal a ledge. That was the best hope. Perhaps he could reach it.

"I'm going up to see if there's a ledge," he announced.

Cabot was ominously silent.

"If there is, I'll get you up. Will you be all right? I'll bring you up afterwards."

Cabot's head raised slightly, as if in farewell. His eyes were dim, he managed to part his lips in a faint, terrifying smile, the smile of a corpse. His teeth were outlined in blood.

"Hang on," Rand told him.

A sickening fear spilled through him as he started, nor did it lessen. He was alone, climbing unprotected. He was worse than alone. He made his way upward, chilled by the malevolence of the wall, imagining it might shed him completely by merely letting loose the entire slab he held to.

The last train had long since gone down from Montenvers. The only eyes at the telescope were those of curious guests of the hotel out for a stroll before dinner. What they saw were details of a magnificent landscape, roseate and still. The light was pure, the sky clear. They, as well as all of creation, were unaware of the chill shadow beneath the overhang and the single figure, heart-empty, hidden within it.

He worked slowly outward, hammering pitons into a narrowing crack and standing in his *étriers*—slings which bore his entire weight. The crack stopped. He searched desperately, there was no place for a piton. Leaning out, he reached around the lip and felt for holds. His hand found one. He might be able to pull himself up, brace one foot against the last piton, and somewhere farther on find another. His fingers felt and refelt the unseen rock. He still had the strength for one big effort. He took a breath and swung out, bent backward, his free hand searching. Nothing. He managed to get a little higher. Nothing. A rush of panic. He was feeling about frantically. At the very top of his reach he found a hold. In tribute to his struggle the rock had relented. He pulled himself up and lay panting. The ledge was two feet wide, uneven, but it was a ledge. He set about bringing up Cabot.

14

The sun had gone down behind Mont Blanc. It was colder. The sky was still light, the small Bleuet stove making tea.

Cabot sat slumped and motionless. The blood had dried on his head and face but his eyes, staring down, were vacant.

The cup passed between battered hands.

"How's your head? It seems to have stopped bleeding."

Cabot bared his black-edged teeth. He nodded slightly.

"I think we're all right for now," Rand told him.

Cabot was silent. After a moment, he murmured, "How's the weather?"

The sky was clear. The first pale star had made an appearance.

"We don't want to fool with the weather," he mumbled. This seemed to exhaust him. He sank into meditation. Rand took the cup from his hand.

In the distance the lights of Chamonix were visible. As it grew darker they became more numerous, distinct. They meant warm meals, conversation, comfortable rooms, all of it unattainable as the stars. It was colder now, it had come quickly, covering the peaks. The long vigil of night began.

Cabot was covered, hands in his pockets, bootlaces loosened. The wall was in shadow, the brown of ancient monuments. A feeling of intense isolation, a kind of claustrophobia came over Rand. It was as if he could not breathe, as if space were crushing him. He fought against it. He thought of where he was and of what might happen. The three cold stars in the belt of Orion shone above. His mind wandered. He thought of condemned men waiting out their last hours, days in California, his youth. His feet were cold, he tried to move his toes. Hours passed, periods of oblivion, of staring at the stars. There were more than he had ever seen. The coldness of the night increased them. They quivered in the thin air. On the dark horizon was the glow of Geneva, constant through the night. A meteor came down like a clot of white fire. An airplane passed to the north. He felt resentment, despair. His eye went down the wall, a thousand feet. He was falling, falling. Cabot never moved; from time to time he moaned.

At first with only the slightest changing of the sky's tone, dawn came. The blue became paler. The stars began to fade. Rand was stiff, weary. The huge dome of Mont Blanc soared into light.

"Jack. Wake up." He had to shake him. Cabot's eyes flickered. They were the eyes of a man who could do nothing, who was dissolute, spent. "It's daylight."

"What time is it?"

"Five-thirty. Beautiful morning in France." His fingers numb, he somehow lit the stove and got out food. Without seeming to, he tried to examine the inert figure.

"I feel better," Cabot unexpectedly said.

Rand looked at him.

"Do you think you can make it down?"

"What?" There was a pause. "No." He was like a powerful beast that has fought and is bloody and torn, seems killed but somehow comes to its feet. "Not down," he said. "I'm all right. I can make it."

"I don't think so."

"I can make it," Cabot insisted.

"The hardest part's ahead."

"I know."

Rand said no more. As he was putting things away and sorting out gear, he tried to think. Cabot was strong, no doubt of it. He seemed in control of himself for the moment. They had come a long way.

"You're sure?" he finally said.

"Yeah. Let's go on."

At first he could not tell, the start was slow. They were stiff from the long hours and the cold. Rand was leading. Soon he saw that Cabot could barely climb. He would simply stay in one spot as if asleep.

"Are you all right?"

"I'm just taking a little rest."

They proceeded with frightening slowness, as one does with a novice. From time to time Cabot would make a gesture: it's all right, I'll just be a minute, but it was nearly always five or ten. Rand had to pull him up with the rope.

They had passed the *bloc coincé* and begun an inside corner where two great slabs of rock met like an opened book. It seemed they were not really here, they were part of some sort of game. They were going through the motions of climbing, that was all. But they could not go down. The time to have done that was earlier, not after they had struggled up an additional five hundred feet. They were near the place where the first party to climb the face had retreated, going around to the north side and descending. Exactly where that was, Rand did not know. He looked for the bolts that had been placed years before but never found them.

They came to a wide slab, chillingly exposed. The holds were slight, hardly more than scribed lines. There was no place to put in a piton. As he went out on it, Rand could feel a premonition, a kind of despair becoming greater, flooding him. It is belief as much as anything that allows one to cling to a wall. He was thirty minutes crossing as many feet, certain as he did that it was in vain.

"It's not as bad as it looks," he called.

Cabot started. He moved very slowly, he was moving by inches. A third of the way across, he said simply,

"I can't make it."

"Yes, you can," Rand said.

"Maybe there's another way."

"You can do it."

Cabot paused, then tried again. Almost immediately, his foot slipped. He managed to hold on.

"I can't," he said. He was done for. "You'll have to leave me here."

Silence.

"No, come on," Rand told him.

"I'm going back. You go on. Come back for me."

"I can't," Rand said. "Look, come on," he said casually. He was afraid of panic in his voice. He did not look down, he did not want to see anything. There is a crux pitch, not always the most technically difficult, where the mountain concedes nothing, not the tiniest movement, not the barest hope. There is only a line, finer than a hair, that must somehow be crossed.

The emptiness of space was draining his strength from him, preparing him for the end. He was nothing in the immensity of it, without emotion, without fear, and yet possessing an anguish, an overwhelming hatred for Cabot who hung there, unwilling to move. Don't give up here, he was thinking. He was willing it, don't give up!

When he looked, Cabot had taken another step.

That evening they were on a ledge far up the face. The overhangs barring the top were above. They had not noticed, until late, the arrival of clouds.

The first gusts blew almost gently but with a chill, a warning of what was to come. In the distance, the crackling of thunder. Rand waited. He tried to disregard it, hoping it would fade. It came again. It was like an air raid drifting closer but still it might pass them by. The clouds were more dense. The Charmoz was disappearing, going dark. Lightning, brilliant in the dusk, was hitting the Brévent. The face of the Dru was still clear, softened by the late hour. The thunder crackled on.

Rand felt helpless. He saw the storm approaching, coming up the valley like a blue wave with scud running before it. He sat watching it fearfully as if it might notice him, veer his way.

Then he heard it, a strange, airy sound all around them. He recognized it immediately, like the humming of bees.

"What's that?" Cabot said.

"Hold on," he warned.

They were in clouds. In a matter of seconds the Dru had gone. They could see nothing. The sound seemed to come from directly overhead and then from closer, almost inside their ears.

"It's getting louder."

Rand did not reply. He was waiting, barely breathing. The mist, the coldness, were like a blindfold. He listened to the eerie, growing hum.

Suddenly the dusk went white with a deafening explosion. Blue-white snakes of voltage came writhing down the cracks.

Lightning struck again. This time his arms and legs shot out from a jolt that reached the ledge. There was a smell of burning rock, brimstone. Hail began to fall. He was clinging to his courage though it meant nothing. He could taste death in his mouth.

Cabot was huddled at his side; he had ended the day moving even more slowly than before. Corpselike in darkness he sat, the earsplitting claps of thunder like the end of the earth itself not even stirring him, a deadweight that was dragging Rand down. There was another flash of lightning. The pathetic figure was clearly visible. Rand stared at it. What he saw he never forgot. It reached across ghosted days to haunt him forever. Half-hidden beneath the bandage, open and gazing directly at him was an eye, a calm, constant, almost a woman's eye that was filled with patience, that understood his despair. Is he alive, Rand wondered? The eye shifted, gazing slightly downward.

An immense explosion. He trembled. There were nine hours until dawn.

15

The storm stopped at midnight. Afterward it froze. Their clothes were wet; the hail had turned into snow. From time to time there came breaks in the cloud when it was possible to see a little, even in darkness, and then the thick wave returned, in absolute silence, sweeping in as if to bury, to obliterate them. Rand was shivering. It was an act of weakness he told himself, but he could not stop.

Finally the sky grew light. There were storms still hanging in the air. Their gear was frozen, the ropes stiff as wire.

They managed to make some tea. In the distance, like hostile armies, an endless line of black clouds was moving. If the weather held, they could try for the top. Rand sipped the tepid, metallic-tasting liquid. He felt empty. He had no resolution, no plan.

For an hour they moved dazedly among the heaps of gear. To straighten it out required the greatest effort. The temptation to sit down and rest was overwhelming. There was snow on every bit of rock, in every crack. The sun was hitting the ridges to the west. Rand was still shivering. It seemed to him to have gotten even colder.

The rock, when he touched it, was like the sides of a deep, sunken wreck. He blew on his fingertips to warm them. His arms and legs felt weary. He heard the sound of birds darting near. For a moment, in fantasy, he dreamed of soaring with them, arms outspread, skimming as they did, the face.

Cabot seemed stronger, he climbed more easily. Above them the mountain had massed its final obstacles. Everything was leaning outward, walls, fragments, dark broken roofs.

"We've got to get above this while the weather is good."

"Tell me," Rand muttered. He felt a strange reversing of things. Instead of being encouraged, he felt drained, as in the final laps when, having given all, one is passed. A single thing sustained him: the summit was near.

"We're going to make it," Cabot said. He was like a captain coming back to the bridge, a bloody figure borne forward to make himself seen.

A final overhang, the last rope-lengths, and they were there. It was nearly noon. Green valleys, glaciers shone below. They were above all but the highest peaks. They stood in silence, too deeply moved to speak. The bivouac spot at the base seemed weeks, even years behind. They still had to descend into a notch and climb some more to go down, but that was not important. The West Face was below them.

Cabot surged ahead. He led the way. He was moving quickly, almost with too much haste, especially on rappels—descent by means of the rope. Descending is always dangerous, the worst seems over.

"What's the rush?" Rand reached out to hold him back.

"Let go."

"You're kicking stuff down."

"Stop worrying," was all he said.

That night they stumbled into the Charpoua hut and slept for eighteen hours. When they reached Montenvers a large man came out of the hotel. He was a reporter from a Geneva paper.

"What happened?" he asked. Cabot looked like the victim of a fight. "Were you hit by rockfall? When? How high up were you?"

He spoke calmly, intimately. He wrote down nothing. He knew the mountains well, having climbed himself. There was an ease about him, that of an aristocrat who has been out in the garden and is wearing old clothes. He knew the entire history of the Dru and how it had been climbed. His eye was sharp, his nose even more so.

Ils livraient leurs vies à la montagne—they bared their lives to the mountain, he would write, *les étalant à son pied*. They laid them at its feet.

The climb was one thing, its confirmation by such a man was another.

That night at dinner in Chamonix, Cabot sat in a yellow sport shirt open at the neck. The bandage was white on his darkened face. He had asked for a table in the back. He had a slight headache, he admitted, but he was elated.

"The best climbing writer in Europe," he said. "I never thought he'd be up there."

"How did that happen?" Rand asked.

Cabot shrugged, "They hear about these things." He was pouring out wine. "He knows the Dru. If he writes about you, that's all you can ask." He was interrupted by the handshake of a noted guide who had made many first ascents. Rand's hand was grasped as well. "Thank you. *Merci*."

"Who was that?" Carol asked.

Glory fell on them lightly like the cool of the evening itself.

Carol was gazing at her husband. "I did expect you to take better care of him," she said.

"I never thought we'd make it," Rand confessed.

"You must have."

"It was foolish."

"No, it wasn't," Cabot said. His face was discolored and blue on one side, handsome on the other, like halves of a personality. "It would have been foolish if we died."

"Yeah, I know. It was superb," Rand murmured.

"Wait and see."

"He was lucky it hit him in the head," Carol remarked. "It could have hurt him."

They had a big dinner, over which they lingered. Cabot was telling all he remembered: nothing from the time he was hit until he said, go on, come back for me, and Rand had told him simply, I can't. Then came the storm. Carol was listening vaguely, her glass had been emptied. There is a drunkenness that seems like wisdom.

"What're you talking about?" she said.

"I'm telling about the storm."

"The same one?"

"Don't interrupt," he said.

Disconsolately she leaned her head on Rand. He could smell her hair, feel her warmth, it was calm, unending, like fields which stretched out of sight. She'd been waiting for her husband for four nights and days.

"The storm," she muttered. "Isn't it over yet?"

"Oh, what's the use?" he said.

"How's your head? Looks awful."

He seemed not to hear.

"Did you see Noyer come over and shake our hands?" he said.

"Is that who it was?"

"Was, is, and will be." Noyer was famous, like Lachenal and Terray.

"Let's go home," she said. "I'm sleepy."

"Let's go," Rand agreed. His happiness had passed its limit. He was tired. He wanted to lie beneath the stars, look up at them, no nearer or farther away than they had been two nights before. As he stood, the chair fell over. The waiter who was a climber himself hurried to pick it up.

"Good night," he said to them in English.

Rand turned at the door. He was tall, eccentric, haggard. At that moment, though he did not realize it, he was launched on a performance which would become irreversible as time went by. On his face were weariness and the haze of ordeal. He waved an arm.

"Yeah, good night," he said. "Keep the change."

16

He was famous, or nearly. There was a tent, people knew, somewhere back in the trees where like a fugitive he had a few possessions, those he needed, rope strewn in dense coils at his feet, heaps of pitons, boots. Almost less than ever was known about him now. There were stories that missed him completely, like confused shots fired in the dark.

He became even more elusive, at least for a time. It only fed the rumors. Every tall, dirt-glazed American was thought to be him. He was seen and talked to in places where he'd never so much as set foot.

A passion for climbing had come over him. As soon as he finished one, he was ready to start another. He climbed the Blaitière with Cabot and then went back with Bray to the Dru and did the regular route. He was either insatiate or absolutely exhausted but then would rise fresh the next day. He was swept up in it entirely as if for the very first time. When he climbed, life welled up, overflowed in him. His ambitions had been ordinary, but after the Dru it was different. A great, an indestructible happiness filled him. He had found his life.

The back streets of town were his, the upper meadows, the airy peaks. It was the year when everything beckons, when one is finally loved. The newspaper clippings were folded and put away. He pretended to scorn them. He kept them despite himself. The true form of legend, he believed, was spoken. He did not want to be catalogued, he said, read and discarded like sports scores and crimes.

"Everyone's written about their climbs," Cabot argued, "Whymper, Hillary, Terray. How else would you know about them?"

"What about the ones we don't know?"

"For instance?"

"Have you ever heard the way they climbed the Walker? Three of them came over from Italy, they didn't even know where it was. They asked the guardian at one of the huts, where are the Grandes Jorasses? Up there, he said. That's how they found it. I don't know if it's true; it's what they say."

"It's only in about ten books. It was Ricardo Cassin," Cabot said.

"I can't explain it. It wouldn't mean as much if I'd read it."

"How do you know?"

It was morning as they sat there, the light still new. Unknown sentinels stood distant, pale. He could have them, he had only to go forth. He was like the sun, touching remote peaks, they awoke to his presence. The thought of it made him reckless. He felt an immense strength. He saw an immortal image of himself high among the ridges—he was willing to die to achieve it.

"I don't want anybody to know how we climbed the Dru, only that we did it. Let them imagine the rest."

"That's nice, but there are a thousand climbers out there," Cabot gestured vaguely.

"So?"

"Only the names of a handful are going to last."

"That's too much like everything else," Rand said. The confusion of what he was feeling kept him from speaking. What he had done, what he would do, he did not want explained. Something was lost that way. The things that were of greatest value, that he had paid so much for, were his alone.

He felt solitary, deep, like a fish in a river, mouth closed, uncaught, glistening against the flow. He saw himself at forty, working for wages, walking home in the dusk. The windows of restaurants, the headlights of cars, shops being closed, all of it part of a world he had never surrendered to, that he would defy to the end.

Late in the season Remy Giro took him to the home of a man named Vigan. It was in an old, established section overlooking the town. Henri Vigan was past forty, familiar in mountaineering circles although only a passable climber himself. He had inherited some factories from his father; they were near Grenoble. He greeted Rand warmly.

"I'm so pleased to meet you," he said. He was open in manner, generous, a man one likes on sight. "You're a native of Chamonix, I think, more than I am. *Vous parlez français?*"

"He doesn't speak. He's a wolf," Remy said. "He lives a secret life, he travels alone."

"All the better," Vigan remarked.

"An Alpha wolf. The leader."

"That's what I imagined. What can I get you to drink?" Vigan asked.

The edge of Rand's beard had burned pale with the summer. His lips shone in its halo. He accepted a glass of wine.

"Let me introduce you to some of my friends," Vigan said.

Confident faces, unrecallable names. The guests were scattered in groups throughout the house. Some seemed to know him, at least who he was, others not to care. They were talking, laughing, at ease. All this had existed when he was sweeping floors up behind the Hôtel Roma, when he fell into bed at Christmas drunk from a bottle of wine. He wanted to avenge himself. He could not be had so cheaply. He was not theirs for a handshake and a compliment. Then he heard,

"Catherin, I think you know . . ."

"Yes," she said, "thank you." She shook hands. She apologized for it with a helpless gesture. "So frog," she explained.

Languid, graceful, she was the salesgirl from Remy's shop. He was unnerved without knowing why.

"I didn't know you spoke English," was all he could say.

"Yes. A little. Some." Her teeth were narrow and white. Her shyness, which he had not noticed before, which had not existed, was extreme. "That was quite an adventure you had on the Dru. Your friend was very lucky."

"Oh, you heard about that?"

She didn't reply. It was as if she disapproved of the inanity of his answer.

"Is he still here?" she finally said. "I haven't seen him."

"He went to Zermatt. He's doing the Matterhorn."

"And you?"

"Me?"

"You didn't go?"

"I decided to stay here."

They were interrupted by Vigan who returned with someone he wanted to introduce. There was some conversation, mostly about the excellence of the season and certain routes climbed so often that excrement was a problem on them, a new objective danger, they lightly agreed.

Catherin, he saw, had wandered into the garden. It was the

hour of evening when, viewed from Les Tines, the Dru is bathed in a vast, almost rose-colored light. The swallows were circling. The last, melancholy sounds of a tennis match drifted up through the pines from the Mont Blanc Hotel. The unhurried way she had left, the possibility of its meaning, that there was someone with her, someone she had returned to, filled Rand with bewilderment, almost sorrow.

He was relieved to find her alone. She was gazing out over the town, the lights of which were just beginning to appear.

"Tell me something," he said, "why did you pretend you didn't speak English?"

"I didn't pretend." She was reserved, polite. She was interested in certain things and those things only. "Why did you decide to stay here instead of going with your friend?"

"I had no plans."

"That's it, you see. Neither did I." She had a slow smile, one reluctantly given. He had no idea what she thought of him or what she was thinking at all.

17

She lived near the cable car station in a house with stone gateposts and an iron fence. It had been a large villa but there had been a decline in its status, like the palaces taken over by troops in a revolution. It contained a number of ill-defined apartments. The walls were bare, the plaster faded.

They drove back from an evening in Argentière, it was their first. He knew much more about her. Her father was English. She liked to joke. At the same time she kept a certain distance—it was like a dance. He might touch her, she would not protest, but she would do no more than patiently submit.

"You're very strange," he told her.

"No, I'm not strange," she said. "I'm quite ordinary."

"I don't believe it."

"Too ordinary."

"Then what am I?"

"I don't know."

"You must have an opinion."

"Not yet," she said simply.

"Have you always lived in Chamonix?"

"Oh, no. I just came here for fun. I liked it, I liked the people." She had stopped the car. "This is where I live," she commented.

He turned his head. There was a ghostly building set back from the street.

"It's a big house."

"There are three families in it."

"It must be big. Can I come in?"

"Oh . . . I don't think so."

"Why not?"

"Really, it's not that interesting."

"The house?"

"Me," she said.

"Just for a few minutes."

They walked to the door. It was heavy, the top was glass with iron bars. She fumbled with some keys.

"Let me go in first."

The door closed behind them. She went up the stairs. In the room she turned on a light.

"There. You see. That's all there is."

He attempted to embrace her but she turned away.

"What is it?" he asked.

"Do you really want to?"

"No, I'm just kidding."

"I'm very flat up here," she said simply. "Practically a man."

"I don't care."

After a moment or two she began to take off her shirt. There was resignation in her movements. She turned off the light and stepped from the last of her clothes. On the main highway beyond the window traffic flowed past. They lay in her narrow bed.

He seemed urgent, overpowering, to her. She had no desires of her own. She had abandoned them, she accepted his. His intensity almost frightened her, his abruptness. As soon as it was over he fell asleep.

In the morning a sun like searchlights was pouring into the room. She returned from somewhere with a small white cup in each hand. Naked down to the sheet that crossed his waist, he was sitting up in bed. His torso seemed to taunt her. It was almost as smooth as hers.

Familiar sounds of morning, cups and indolent spoons. He was less interested in her this morning, she saw. Her heart was beating sadly. Around his neck was a pale green string of narrow beads; she saw them in the mirror as she dressed.

"You can stay if you like," she said.

He watched her silently.

"I have to go to work," she said. She gave a fleeting smile, as if required.

He lay in bed. A womanly smell still clung to it. He could hear footsteps elsewhere in the house, they seemed aimless. Opening and closing of doors. The empty cups were on the floor. As if it had suddenly started, he noticed the ticking of her clock. He felt luxurious. He took himself for granted, his legs, his sexual power, his fate. A consciousness that had faded came into life. It was like a film when the focus is blurred and shifting and all at once resolves; there leaps forth a hidden image, incorruptible, bright.

When he went by the shop he said a few whispered words to her. Her expression softened, she did not reply. The thing that betrayed her was an unexpected, childish gesture. After he had gone, elated by his visit, she took hold of the end of the counter, leaned back and pulled herself dreamily forward, leaned back and did it again.

"Vous êtes bien?" Remy inquired.

"Très bien."

18

The curtain had fallen. September was a month of good weather and beautiful light, but the town was nearly empty, everyone had gone.

"I wouldn't mind staying around," Bray lamented, "but Audrey's coming to Geneva. I said I'd meet her." She was his girlfriend. "This is the only time she could get away. Besides, my money's gone. I'm not like you, I can't live off women."

He'd been driving Catherin's little car around town.

"So, I'm afraid that's it," Bray said. He could have been a small-time crook with nerve and a taste for cheap display. He liked to smoke big cigars after dinner, drink Martell. The mountains had saved him.

He hadn't the imagination which is indispensable to greatness. Supreme climbs need more than courage, they need inspiration. He was a sergeant in the ranks—perhaps, in tumultuous times, he might be a colonel, one who wears his blouse unbuttoned and gets drunk with the men.

Audrey was a nurse. She had the characteristics of her class, she was scornful, outspoken. She hated foul language and foreign cooking and was indifferent to sports. Her youth, in part, softened these things. In many English women there is, despite reputation, a strong sensuality, even if denied. Her face was unfriendly, but it was the extraordinary skin which made her body luminous that Bray dreamed of. His letters were filled with an erotic imagery one would never expect.

"Why don't you come to England? Tear yourself away. There's work. You could work with me."

"Doing what?" Rand said.

"Plastering. It has a tradition. O'Casey was a plasterer."

"Who?"

"O'Casey. He wrote plays. You've heard of him. It doesn't matter. We'll throw in a little culture, too."

"Maybe I'll come."

"We'll be back here in December, anyway," Bray said.

"What for?"

"The Eiger. Cabot asked me to come." He was obviously pleased. "He didn't tell you?"

"No." After a pause, he added, "What about the Eiger?"

Suddenly Bray was embarrassed. He realized something was wrong.

"Ah, well, I thought . . . I thought you knew. He's going to do a winter ascent."

"Oh, yeah?" Rand managed to say.

"I thought you knew all about it."

Rand felt as if he had been slapped in the face.

"No," he said.

"Sorry."

"That's all right," Rand said. "Tell me about it."

He hardly heard the words, they were slipping by. It was

going to be like Scott . . . his push to the pole . . . bivouacs prepared in advance, bunkers, with two or three weeks of food so that they could ride out any storm. The BBC would be filming.

"I see." He suddenly hated Bray. The feeling that something had been stolen from him was crushing his heart.

"I suppose everybody wants to climb it," Bray said lamely.

"They don't want to climb it, they want to *have* climbed it." He was searching his pockets for money. "Here," he said, putting some on the table, "pay for mine."

He walked out into the empty afternoon. The sun threw light against the buildings. He felt utterly abandoned, ill.

"What's wrong?" Catherin cried.

Desperation glittered from him. He was slumped on the bed.

"Don't you feel well?" she said.

"I'm all right." He lay back.

"What is it?" she said.

"It's nothing. Cabot is going to do a climb, that's all."

"He can climb. Is that bad?"

"He's going to do the Eiger."

"Please, what is it? You look as if you were going to die."

That night he lay awake while over and over in his mind turned the same bitter thoughts. The room seemed small. He longed to be up in the woods, alone. The sky would calm him, the icy galaxies. He felt he'd been caught away from home. He wanted to go to ground.

He remembered the girl from Kauai who had cut his hand. She believed in the occult. She was humorless, intense. Write down the names, she had said, of your three closest friends and I will circle the name of your deadliest enemy.

19

The autumn days have a fever. The sun is departing, it gives forth all that remains. The warmth is mysterious, it carries a message: farewell.

Catherin saved him. In her small car they drove off on weekends, Aix-les-Bains once, Chambéry. In the countryside they pulled off the road and descended, feet slipping, a steep embankment. The hillside was facing the sun, not a house, not a person to be seen. The fallen leaves had drifted deep, they came to the knee. They ate from a basket she had prepared and lay sprawled afterward, bees feeding on the remnants of the meal.

An hour went by, an hour and a half. Slowly Rand sat up. Catherin's eyes swam open for a moment.

"Oh, God," she breathed.

"What is it?"

"I'm still asleep."

"Wake up."

"It's so hard," she said weakly. "When I die, I hope I don't have to wake afterwards. It would be so difficult."

He knelt beside her. She leaned against him. There was a faint plop—two moths, gray as wood with one spot of dazzling blue, had fallen, attached to one another. They did not move.

"You see?" she said.

There was a stream below. They walked down through blue and violet flowers, scattered, abandoned by summer. Then through a dry orchard. At the far end a goat, all white, was staggering about on its hind legs to eat from the branches. It would be cold that winter. The mice had left the pastures. The leaves were already down.

They looked back. Half-hidden in the earth were long, stone walls built to retain the hillside. The sun was fading. The white of the car glinted far above.

The last rites of autumn. They walked up slowly. She was out of breath; she had to stop. He carried her the rest of the way, not in his arms but over his shoulder, cheek against her haunch. She didn't struggle. She hung quietly, touching him as if he were a horse.

In Annecy they walked by the lake. An empty dock stretched out into the water. The varnished boats creaked. He lived an entire life in Annecy, in a hotel with an iron balcony and the letters H-O-T-E-L fixed to it. The television cost a franc. A bottle of Perrier stood outside the window. They went to bed at midnight. Her bracelets crashed on the table glass.

"Too much to drink," she managed to announce. The windows were open. An occasional car, driving too fast, zoomed along the street.

Dawn turned the mountains dark. The sky was pale, the hour unknown. He went out on the balcony. Annecy was blue. The buildings had a phantom form, they were rising as if from the sea. A single eye looked up at him from among the bedclothes, an eye still stained with makeup. A drugged voice said,

"What are you doing up in the middle of the night?"

A lifetime and more. He began to actually see France, not just a mountain village filled with tourists, but the deep, invisible center which, if entered at all, becomes part of the blood. Of course, he did not know the meaning of the many avenues Carnot or boulevards Jean Jaurès, the streets named Gambetta, Hugo, even Pasteur. The pageant of kings and republics was nothing to him, but the way in which a great civilization preserves itself, this was what he unknowingly saw. For France is conscious of its brilliance. To grasp it means to sit at its table, sleep beneath its roofs, marry its children.

Immortal mornings. His genitals were heavy, like the dark, smooth stone carved by the Eskimos. They had a gravity, a denseness he could not believe. He drew aside the sheet. She was naked. Her hair was strewn across the pillow. She was like a drowned woman, she was sunk in bed like a burial at sea. He placed a hand on her, proprietary, calm. The first cars were driving past. Someone's footsteps echoed in the street.

This love was the act of one person, it was not shared. He was like a man in a boat on a wide lake, a perfectly still lake at dawn. There was no sound except that of oars in the oarlocks, creaking, creaking, a man alone in a boat that slowly begins to shudder, to cry. Afterwards they lay close, like comrades.

His hair was like hers. His arm lay near her side, the muscle sleeping, the light barely tracing it.

"Are we going back to Chamonix?" she asked.

"Let's keep moving. Let's stay ahead of them."

"I'd like to take you to Paris." She was stroking the arm with her fingers. "I want to show you off."

"Where would we stay?" He was filled with a sublime weariness, as if he had just fallen into bed after an unforgettable party. "What about your job?"

"Oh, Remy won't care. It's very slow now, anyway." She

seemed to drop off to sleep. "I have some money," she said after a pause. "We'll have a marvelous time."

They rose at noon to look for a restaurant. They were famished.

The apartment was on a small street off the avenue du Maine. They arrived in the evening, a blue evening the color of storms and drove along the river in streams of traffic, then through dense neighborhoods. The early darkness was lit by storefronts. The buses were roaring by. There was an electric thrill to the city seen at this hour and for the first time. He was dazzled. The trees still held their enormous leaves. Outside restaurants there were stands selling oysters, the baskets tilted forward for customers to see. The streets were crowded. The city was singing to him, flowing like a great, unimagined dream.

There were only two rooms, strangely empty of furniture as if someone had just moved out. A kitchen, a long, narrow bath with red walls. The water limped into the tub, a gas heater roared to life when the hot was turned on. There were photographs and invitations stuck in the mirror. The refrigerator, there being no space elsewhere, was in the front room.

The woman who owned it, Madame Roberts, came around the next day. She had a long mane of hair and beautiful shoes. She admitted to being forty-five. It was her daughter who lived here normally and who was away.

"In Rome," she explained. "She's decided to go to school. She took a lot of things. I hope you can be comfortable." She had a very frank gaze. "But you're used to sleeping in worse places, aren't you?" she said to Rand. "Catherin has told me about you, your fantastic life. You're not an intellectual, are you?"

"An intellectual?" he said.

"Good, I'm sick of them." She had strong, white teeth, she brushed them with salt. She owned a shop across the river: imported clothing, accessories, things like that—she'd started it herself.

"It's very nice. I have a certain clientele. Catherin knows. I treat them very well. I have good things." Her presence was rich, full of life. She rummaged in her handbag for a cigarette. Her legs, in stockings that had a metallic sheen, were crossed above the knee. She'd been a mannequin, that was how she started.

"The first time I had absolutely no confidence. There was a woman in the dressing room who had experience. She saw how frightened I was. She took me aside. Just remember, she said, when you go out there—you are young and beautiful and they are shit. Everything I did, I did for myself," she said. "No one gave me anything. My husband gave me half the apartment when we were divorced. He put up a brick wall. He kept the living room and kitchen and I got the bedroom and bath."

Her business she conducted like the famous courtesans. The men who came to her she classified as *payeurs*, *martyrs*, or *favoris*. "As long as they don't compare notes. Being a mannequin was a help; I developed a taste for luxury." Her voice was powerful and flowing. She used it like a stream of water. Her laugh was hoarse, the laugh of a free woman. "I developed a taste for it, but I didn't let it ruin me," she said.

Paris was filled with such women, he saw them on the streets, in buses, everywhere. Students, married women, extravagant faces in bars and cafés. In the windows of *parfumeries* gleamed seductive advertisements for the care of the breasts and skin. His eye lingered on them like a young husband looking at whores.

In a bar off Boulevard St. Michel there was a girl with her

eyes outlined in black and a bright silk scarf wrapped around and around her swanlike neck.

"Who is it, someone you know?" Catherin asked—she was leafing through a magazine. He began to read over her shoulder. It was November. Nights were cold, but days still fair. Paris was opening itself to him, he thought.

There were friends of Catherin's. "*Bonsoir*," one said, extending her hand. Her name was Françoise. A dark-haired man was behind her, he shook hands disinterestedly.

"This is Michel," she said as they sat down. "Michel has lived in England. You're English?" she asked Rand.

"No," he said.

"*Américain*," Michel commented wearily. "*C'est vrai?*"

"That's right."

Michel nodded. It was too simple. "*Vous êtes grimpeur?*" he said offhandedly. Françoise had told him.

"Speak English," she said.

"*Je ne parle pas anglais.*"

"Yes, you do."

"It's too difficult," he said. He then told a story in French about a party he had gone to in London. A girl had come over and asked why he was off by himself. He told her he was French, he didn't speak English. Oh, she said, in two months he would speak it fluently. He'd been there two years, he told her. She didn't talk to him again.

"*Oh, tu m'énerves*," Françoise said.

They sat in silence.

"What have you climbed?" he asked in French. "I had a good friend who was a climber."

"Who?" said Françoise.

Michel said, "You don't know him. He was in the army. He liked the army, he was one of those, but he got in some trouble and had to leave. Afterwards, he began to climb seriously. First not far from Paris, then down at Marseilles, and in the Alps. He was very strong, very pure. In some ways he was like a child."

Rand was watching him suspiciously. Michel was aware of it. He spoke more slowly, unaffectedly, as if to them all.

"He began to climb the most difficult peaks in Europe. Climbing is more than a sport. That's true, isn't it? *Ça dure toujours*—it lasts forever."

They were listening in silence. A sensation of panic had come over Rand. He could not believe these sentences were following one upon the other. Michel's eyes were looking directly into his.

Rand smiled. He wanted to break this spell, to show that he was not subject to it.

"Who's this friend?"

"I can only tell you," Michel went on, "that his dream was to become one of the greatest climbers of all time."

"Is that right?" A confusion was rising in him. He had a sudden, strange sense of isolation, as if all the people surrounding him, sitting at nearby tables, talking, laughing, were part of what was being enacted, were even aware of it.

"I don't know anything about climbing," Michel said then. He was confiding, he wanted to become a friend. "I saw him not long ago. Something had happened to him. I don't know. I hadn't seen him for almost a year. He had left his wife, he wasn't working. Still he felt if he climbed one more mountain, everything would somehow fall into place. It was like a drug. He constantly had to have more and more, and the doses had to be bigger."

Rand said nothing. He stared coldly.

"He was always an idealist. He had great inner strength, more than you've ever seen. But something had changed in him, I could see it in his face. He had done everything and he was still unhappy. Two weeks ago . . ."

Rand's heart was pounding. The panes of illusion were slipping from his life. He felt himself disappearing.

"I don't like this story," Catherin interrupted.

"I don't like it, either. Furthermore, I don't believe it," Françoise said.

"But it's true," Michel said.

"I don't think so."

"Then I don't tell it."

"Go ahead, finish it," Rand said.

Michel smiled.

"Go ahead."

"Two weeks ago, on an easy climb, he fell to his death."

"Why don't you talk about something you know?" Françoise complained.

"I said I knew nothing. That's what makes it fascinating. I'm interested in the psychology of it. It's a story of someone completely unlike me. I don't have the courage. I don't have the slightest bit. Intelligence, that's all."

"Too much intelligence and not enough of something else," she said.

"Here is a man with courage." He indicated Rand. "He doesn't like me. Look."

"Oh, you are boring!" Françoise cried.

"Look, he wants to fight. He wants to take his fists and smash what he doesn't like. That's the American spirit."

"Will you shut up?"

"Why don't you hit me?" he challenged.

Rand stared at him.

"What's wrong? Can't you speak?"

"I'm leaving. Come on," Françoise said.

"But the story was true!" he called out as they stood up. "You know that, don't you? You see? He knows."

20

"Michel! Michel is a *pédé* and a drunk. You should have thrown him into the street," Colette Roberts said. She was having a hurried coffee before opening her shop. In the morning her face had a visible weariness like the city itself. There was the flat, winter light, the drabness.

"Michel is not even French," she said. "He's a Polish Jew. Your hair, you know, looks like the rumpled tail of a big rooster."

He felt worthy in her presence, alive. She was like a mirror in which he saw himself perfectly. She knew how to manage things; she was not an amateur in life.

"Where is Catherin?" she asked.

"She had to go to the bank."

"Come by and have a drink this evening. I have a friend coming from Nice." Someone entering the bar greeted her. She nodded, smiled. "I'm late," she suddenly realized. "Come at six." She dropped some coins on the counter. She was a woman who would never be down for long.

In the mornings he read, sitting near the window, a copy of the *Tribune* a day or two old. In the afternoon they would go out.

The tunnels of the Métro were filled with slogans. The talk in the cafés was always political, fierce. On the kiosks were posters of scandal, exposé. France was like a great, quarreling family, the Algerians, the old women with their dogs, the people in restaurants, the police—a huge, bickering family bound eternally by hatred and blood.

There were afternoons of emerging soft-eyed from movies and walking past the gray vaults of the Montparnasse Cemetery, feet cold, to reach home. Afternoons when light snow was falling from nowhere and the city was blue as ice, the sound of traffic far off. Or in cafés, talking and watching the crowd. A woman in a green silk shirt sat alone at a nearby table. She was reading something taken from her handbag. A timetable. Suddenly her eyes opened wide. She was talking to herself, astonished. She rose, put on her coat, and ran out.

Secret afternoons, undisclosed. Silence sealing the windows. In the filtered light she seemed mythic, gleaming, as if for the first time the marvel of a body was revealed. She was wearing only her underpants. The blood was beating slowly in his neck. Samurai hours. The shutter of a camera clicked.

"Will they develop these?"

"Of course," she said.

"I doubt it. They'll steal them."

She was sitting cross-legged on the bed when he came out of the bath, lazily playing solitaire. The kings and queens had names printed on the cards, the jacks were Hector, Lahire. He lay beside her, watching.

"Is this what they mean by wasting your life?"

"You're joking," she said.

Great as it was, the city could not sustain him. Faint in its streets, its chill, winter passages, came a lonely sound, small, incessant, something being chipped away bit by bit. The pale sky only made it louder. It was the sound of an ice ax, Cabot's. It would not stop.

At four in the morning he woke. The sky, the streets were absolutely silent. He could not sleep. Somewhere, half in dream, the dark wedge of the Eiger loomed in an empty sky. It had snowed in the mountains. The roads were white, the valleys blanketed. A strong wind was blowing. Snow poured down the face in streams.

He had entered a room where Cabot lay dying. He could not believe it, he was numb, but when he saw the coffin and the face within it, the sealed eyes, the fine hair, suddenly he was felled by grief, knocked to his knees. He was weeping unashamedly.

Catherin was trying to wake him.

"What is it?" she said. He could not answer. "What happened? You were crying out."

He lay there with his arms around her. Neither of them could sleep.

21

The Eiger is the great wall of Europe. It exists in a class by itself. Six thousand feet high, twice the height of the Dru, and more treacherous. Its color is black except for the snow which in winter clings everywhere, hiding the fields of ice. The climbing is difficult, the danger from storm and falling rock extreme.

The first attempts were all fatal though they forged the way. Men fell or froze to death, their bodies remaining on the face, grotesquely, for long periods of time. In 1938 it was finally climbed.

There is an old hotel, the Kleine Scheidegg, not far from the base. The rooms are comfortable, the downstairs is filled with photographs of those who have made the climb. Above, so immense that it cannot be seen, the mountain soars.

They were all staying at the hotel—Cabot had gotten five climbers, he was trying to find a sixth. Early in the morning, before dawn, they would leave for the foot of the wall, trudging across frozen fields. At night they returned exhausted.

"You know anyone else we could get?" he asked Bray.

"I know someone in Paris."

Cabot glanced at him. "Is there anyone you know in England?"

Bray said, "Not for this."

It was like war in a city besieged. All day they fought furiously. At night they slept in their beds.

Carol was there; she was the leading woman. Audrey, who came in January, was pale beside her. In the evening, if no one was back, they ate together, sometimes with the television crew. A chain-smoking man named Peter Barrington was the producer.

"Huh! Damned cold today," he said, batting together his mittened hands. "Glad I'm not up there. Where's our pilot this morning?"

He'd made films on architecture and English poets. Then he'd gone to Nepal, which made him the expert on mountaineering, he said with a captious air. He knew all the jargon, however. He used it freely. Cabot, he secretly called "The Strangler." Much of his time was spent in the bar at a table with an overflowing ashtray—he was waiting for certain equipment, for the weather to improve, for a call from London.

"Good morning, Peter," they would say.

"Beautiful morning, isn't it? What do you suppose we should do today? Take a few more pictures of the mountain?"

"We could do that."

"What are they up to today?"

It had been slow going. Cabot had broken his thumb in a twenty-foot fall. It hadn't stopped him; he kept at it, doing as much as anyone, even more. He was the only one who believed they would reach the top. The others, were mere soldiers, automatons.

The face was completely frozen. It prevented any rockfall to speak of but the cold was intense. Avalanches of snow were frequent. Slowly, with unwavering determination, a route, completely new, was being pushed up. Fixed ropes were left in place so that going up and down could be managed quickly. The focus of effort was always the highest point.

By mid-January they were halfway up the wall. Two well-stocked bivouacs dug out of snow had been established, bunkers Cabot called them. They had to make a third. The fixed ropes would then be taken down and, starting from the bottom, one man would attempt the climb. That had not been the original idea—it had come to him as time went on. From the third bunker it would be one sustained push, carrying food and equipment with him. He would climb to the summit alone.

But the third bunker defied them. They were on a very steep part of the face. There was no snow, only solid ice that had to be chipped away inch by inch. Their hands were frozen, their feet. Three hundred feet above was a place which looked slightly better.

There's going to be no third bloody bivouac, Bray was thinking. There's going to be nothing. He was exhausted, his fingers were burning with cold. He could feel nothing in his feet. He was afraid of losing his toes, having them freeze, but it did no good to think of it. He hated the clear, cold weather that had come two days before. He hated Cabot. Ten more, he muttered to himself as he chopped at the ice. Small slivers shot off like spray. Every other blow did nothing. Nine. Ten. He paused. All right, another ten, he vowed.

"How are you doing up there?"

Cabot was almost directly below. Bray could see the top of his head. He didn't answer.

"How's it going?" Cabot called.

"I can't do it," Bray muttered.

"What?"

"My hands are freezing."

After a while he came down.

"How far did you get?"

"Nowhere. It's like cutting steel."

"Let me try."

Cabot went up using the jumars—devices with one-way ratchets in them. Pushed up alternately, they had long, nylon loops to stand in. He went up smoothly, spinning around slowly on the taut rope. Soon there was the distant, rhythmic sound of his ax. It was ten in the morning. They'd been at work since dawn.

"They're predicting good weather. They expect it to last through the week," Barrington said. "It's coming from the east."

They had come back to the hotel. It was too cold to stay on the face and not that much time was lost in going up the ropes. It could be done in darkness.

"Incredible cold. I don't know how you do it," Barrington said. "Can you see a place for the last bunker?"

"Not yet," Cabot said. "We'll find one."

Carol had gone to Munich to talk to some television people. The curtain had not risen for the final act but it would not be long. Something had been sacrificed in the way it all was arranged. The climb was not classic—it was, in a sense, corrupt. The conquest of heights by any means and for whatever purpose is questionable. Of course, this was never brought up.

The involvement was already too great and Cabot was too compelling a figure. He was the kind of man who did not conform to standards, he created them.

"It's just that if we could take advantage of the good weather . . . ," Barrington said.

"Well, we're trying."

"Because afterwards, it could be . . . difficult."

"Look, would you like to go up there yourself?" Cabot said.

Barrington reddened. "I'm afraid that wouldn't accomplish much."

"No." Cabot suddenly changed his tone—the soup was being served, he drew the plate toward him. "Don't worry," he said. "We'll get it. It's just a little farther."

Bray was two chairs away, hunched over, eating in silence.

"There's the man who's going to do it." It fell on the ears of a sullen acolyte with blistered lips, weary of it all. "He'll do it. And gentlemen in England now a-bed will think themselves accurs'd they were not here, right?"

Bray continued eating as if he hadn't heard. Later Audrey came down. They'd been married in the fall. They hadn't taken a honeymoon, two days in Brighton, that was all.

"You've eaten," she said. "I thought you were going to wait for me." She sat down. "What did you have?"

"I think it was a cutlet."

"God, your face. Look at it."

"What, this?" He touched his lip.

"Are you going up again tomorrow?"

"I suppose so. Ask him."

She turned to Cabot.

"Are you?" She wasn't sure why she disliked him—his cold determination, they all had some of that.

Cabot was tired, too. His face was scalded from the cold. His eyes were red. In the corridor, afterward, he stopped her.

"Don't discourage him," he said. "It's hard up there."

There was music coming from the bar. Along the corridor over their heads passed the sound of someone running. Then laughter, again from the bar. White-aproned cooks were at work in the warmth of the kitchen. Guests sat in front of the television. In the office someone was totaling bills. On the face of the Eiger even the ropes were frozen. They dangled in darkness like pieces of wood.

"Is John really tired?" Cabot said.

"Well, you know he's a fool. He doesn't complain," she said.

"I know."

They sat for a while in the bar. Cabot's blond, scattered hair seemed dull in the subdued light. He was like a derelict seen in the shadows, indistinct, something helpless about him. Perhaps he was asleep.

The next morning they went again. They had decided to stay on the face until they reached the snowfield that seemed to lie above. Bray went first. They had left the hotel in darkness and all the way across the icy fields, a way they had traveled many times, not a word was said. Once Cabot slipped and fell. Bray hadn't turned around.

All day he bore the brunt. They were making their way up an ice-filled crack. It was twenty minutes' work to move a foot. The crack slowly widened, he was braced against its sides. Bray felt he was there alone. A strange feeling came over him, a detachment, almost euphoria, as if he were nothing more than a photograph. The silence beneath him vanished, fear fell away. He kept on working upward. He was clinging to nothing, balanced there somehow. He felt his foot begin to slip. He tried to hold on.

"Tension!" he cried.

The rope tightened. It wasn't enough.

"I'm coming off!" Three thousand feet above the valley he began to fall. He saw it all clearly, he deplored it, he hardly cared.

The rope caught him abruptly. Somehow his leg was entangled in it. He was hanging upside down, ten feet from Cabot.

"Are you all right?"

"I've lost my glove," he said.

Cabot lowered him.

"What happened?"

"Couldn't do it." He was breathing hard, his bare hand thrust inside his jacket. "I couldn't hold on." It was far into the afternoon. The sun had passed its zenith. The sky seemed white. "Next year I'm going back to plastering," he said.

"You sure you're all right?"

Bray nodded. He looked down. Suddenly he felt frightened. His courage had gone. After a while, he asked, "Are you going up to try?"

"You only have one glove."

"Anyway, look at the weather," Bray said. Clouds had appeared in the distance.

He was spent, that much is certain. Late in the day the two figures which had been motionless for hours began to descend. Perhaps the rope had been worn against the ice. Perhaps a rock had cut it. No one would ever know. To those who were watching, a speck of color seemed to free itself and move very slowly, almost to float, down the face. And with it, the cry,

"Someone's fallen!"

Audrey often passed her time in a sitting room where the guests had tea. It was warm there and comfortable. She would talk to people, write postcards, and read. It was pleasant, sitting there, drinking tea, receiving the curious glances of tourists and their identical questions. Where are they? they asked and she would point them out as well as she could.

"Oh, my."

"How far up are they?"

"A long way."

"Doesn't it make you nervous?"

"I don't think about it," she told them.

She had heard nothing. She saw something that frightened her, people were suddenly rising all along the veranda. There was a crowd at the telescope.

"What is it? What's happened?" she asked. She'd been reading. The book lay facedown beside her. As she stood up, she felt unsteady. She could not hear what they were saying, she could not hear anything. It was like a vacuum. In a moment the eyes of the crowd would turn toward her. She was certain of it. "Please. What's happened?" she said.

22

That night it began to snow. In the dusk it fell softly. People were talking at dinner. Waiters glided across the room. Sometime after seven, Cabot, who had been out for hours at the foot of the wall, knocked on the partly open door.

"Come in." It was Barrington's voice. Audrey was sitting in a chair, a cardigan around her shoulders.

"Hello, Jack. Are they all back?" Barrington asked.

Pieces of Bray's equipment were scattered around, boots behind the door, socks drying on the radiator. Cabot sat down. He found it hard to speak.

"We got back a little while ago," he said.

"Is it snowing hard?"

"Pretty hard. One thing that's almost sure," he said, not looking at Audrey, "he was unconscious the whole time."

"How do you know?"

"I was there. I saw it. I saw him hit his head, right at the start."

"You saw that?"

"Yes, that's probably so," Barrington confirmed. "It's very jagged there."

The word disturbed her. "Jagged . . ."

"Lots of outcrops."

"I hope you're right," she said.

They were silent. The immense length of the fall and the helplessness of the climber, falling, filled the room. After a while Barrington rose and left. He would look in later, he said.

"I don't know what to tell you," Cabot finally broke the silence—the shock had been great for him. "The rope . . . it must have caught on something. I can't imagine. It's . . . it could have happened to anyone."

"Don't be silly," she said.

"It was just one of those impossible accidents."

"No, it wasn't. It wasn't an accident. I knew you would kill him," she said. "I knew it the first time I laid eyes on you."

"You don't believe that."

"Oh, yes."

"It's not true."

"Isn't it?" she said. "Oh, yes. He was only a little man, I mean compared to you, but he was loyal, he had a good heart. You could make him do anything. All you had to say was you didn't think he could do it and do it he would go and try. Well, you know that. I've seen you make him. So the rope broke and now he's gone. Last night he was here. He stood right in front of that mirror. He was dead tired, but you'd never get him to stop because he was tired. Now, where is he? I don't even know where he is." She had begun to cry. "You'll go on," she said. "You'll get to the top. You won't even remember him."

"That's not so."

"Oh, yes, it is," she said bitterly.

"Listen, Audrey, it's hard to explain." He paused for a moment. "I didn't make him do anything, he did it for the same reason I did. Nothing can make you do it. You do it because of yourself."

She stood by the window staring out at the snow. She was hugging herself, her arms clasped beneath her breasts.

"I'm sorry but I just don't believe you," she said wearily. The way she was holding herself, as if she could expect nothing more from life, the clothes and cosmetics on the dresser, the pale square of bed reflecting light, these seemed to be speaking for her. The room was warm. The silence was mounting, like a bill that would have to be paid.

"Come and have dinner. You don't want to be alone tonight," he said. "If you like, we'll eat in the bar. I'll ask them to serve us there."

"I don't want to go to the bar."

"It'll do you some good."

"Leave me alone."

He put his arm around her.

"Audrey . . ." He tried to say something else, but nothing came.

She nodded, she didn't know why. She'd begun to cry again, the tears running down her cheeks.

"What's going to happen to me?" she said.

"You'll go back to England."

She looked at him.

"Is that all?" she demanded.

He made a vague gesture.

"Is that all?"

"I'll meet you in five minutes," he said.

She did not answer.

"Are you coming downstairs?"

"Yes," she finally said.

"In a few minutes?"

"Yes."

He did not move. He saw there was no need to. Instead he put his hand on her breast, he had been looking at it for weeks.

"Don't," she said. He felt her shudder but she did not move. "Don't."

He turned her toward him.

It was as if they had spoken, as if it had always been agreed. Carol was still in Munich. The snow fell through the night.

There was a small item at the bottom of the page, CLIMBER KILLED IN FALL. His eye was skipping the words. The blood left his face, he tried to read calmly. *Wengen, Jan. 24. Authorities identified today a 23-year-old English climber who fell 3,000 feet to his death on the Eiger yesterday . . .*

It was Sunday in Paris and cold. Around him people were talking, the television was on. He felt as drained and colorless as the day. Suddenly everything was dreary. He was irritated by French being spoken, by the strangers around him, by the ignorance of the world. He thought of Bray, a little grinning man in a dirty jacket, small hands. Are you coming to England? We'll work together, he said. The two of us. Side by side.

23

Catherin came down the stairway buttoning her coat. He had been waiting for her outside.

They walked toward the center of town. There were people everywhere; Chamonix was filled with the last crowds of winter. Cars passed, spattered with mud.

"Well, what did he say?"

"It's definite," she said.

"Definite?"

"The test is positive."

"I don't understand it. How could that be?"

"It just is," she said.

He was silent. He stared numbly into shop windows as they walked.

"Would you like a coffee?" she asked.

They sat near the back, Rand slumped in his chair.

"Well, I see the news has thrilled you," she remarked.

"It's not that. It's just . . ."

"What?"

"It's just a surprise."

"Well, I'm surprised, too."

"It's not exactly what I was planning on."

"I see that."

The waitress returned with the coffee.

"What *are* you planning on?" Catherin asked. She took three cubes of sugar and dropped them in the tiny cup.

"Not family life."

She said nothing.

"I don't want to be a father."

"How do you know?" She was slowly stirring her coffee. "You'd be a very good father."

"Don't do it," he finally said.

"It's too late."

"What do you mean, too late?"

"It's sixteen weeks."

The number meant nothing to him. He was sure she was lying. "I'd like to know how it happened," he insisted. "How could it?"

"I don't know. Something went wrong."

"What?"

"Is this the investigation? Why didn't you investigate before we started?"

"I can't be a father," he said.

She was silent.

"Perhaps you don't want to marry. That's what you mean."

"Perhaps."

"Yes. I understand."

A terrible heaviness hung on him. He gazed around the room vaguely, as if for a different idea.

"Well, I don't know what to do. *Merde*," she said.

"Catherin, you know what my life is like."

"*Ça veut dire quoi?*" After a while she added, "What do you want? Do you want to go on like you are?"

"You don't go on like you are. A year from now, two years, I won't be the same."

"What will you be?"

"How do you know? I don't want to be tied down."

"You won't be," she said. "I promise. You can always do anything you like."

The words calmed him. He might have accepted them on the spot if she had not been so abject. Besides, she would forget what she was saying now, her instincts as a woman would come out. That was what always happened.

"You want me to get rid of it," she said finally.

Yes, he thought, but for some reason said nothing. There is a moment when the knife must be pushed in coldly, otherwise the victim triumphs. He looked at her, aware that the moment was passing.

"Oh, hell," he muttered.

She knew that she had failed him. She felt helpless, in despair. They sat in silence.

"Talk to me," she pleaded.

He said nothing.

That spring he was seldom in Chamonix. He was up in one refuge hut or another, sometimes for days. It was early in the season. The dormitory rooms were empty, the mattresses side by side. *After 9 P.M. Silence*, commanded the signs.

Occasionally other climbers appeared. They rarely spoke. The huts were still cold from winter, with outdated tariffs pinned on the wall. It was difficult when he came back down. He came less often and stopped at the shop.

"*Ça va?*" he murmured awkwardly. Her shape did not seem to have changed.

"How was it up there?"

"Still a lot of snow."

"So that's where it is," she said.

He failed to smile. As soon as he could, he left, somewhat uneasy about what she might say. He hated parting comments. There was a kind of agreement that they were still somehow together, at least the appearance was maintained. In a town as small as Chamonix things were found out quickly although, in the strictest sense, they were outsiders.

"I'm going up to Argentière," he said one day. "If conditions aren't too good, I might wait around for a while up there, you know?"

"You don't have to hurry back," she said. "I'm not going to be here."

It was like a sudden blow.

"Oh? Where are you going?"

There is a time when one says, I love you more than life itself, I will give you anything. Somehow the feeling of that flickered before her—she was leaving, she had already decided—it was like a last glance back.

"I'm going to Paris," she said.

"Well, I'll see you when you come back."

She did not answer. She was remembering his face for the last time. Her silence frightened him.

"Or will I?" he said.

"No, I don't think so."

Suddenly he was desperate. He was tormented by her. He loved her and this love was choking him. He wanted her and she was leaving.

"What are you going to do in Paris?"

"I'm going to stay with a friend," she told him.

"Who?"

"What difference does it make?"

What difference? It was maddening. All the difference in the world. He tried to make her tell him but she would not.

The friend was Henri Vigan. Catherin had once been his mistress—for two years—and left because he would not marry her. She went back to him. He accepted her willingly. If she wished, he said, he would consider the child as his own.

She settled in Izeaux—Vigan had his box factories near there—in an old house right on the street, built in the days when only an occasional carriage or cart passed by. The outside walls were plain, even drab, but the interior was warm and comfortable as only French country houses can be, with many doors giving onto the garden. There she was happy or at least freed from the difficulty of loving the wrong person. It would be wrong to say she did not think of him, but she did so with less and less frequency.

Vigan was gentle and understanding. He was also flattered to have her back, doubly so since she had come from the arms of a younger, daring man. When she wanted to return to Chamonix to get her clothes, he forbade her.

"I'll have someone collect them and take them up to my house. You can't wear them now, anyway."

He found her more beautiful, as pregnant women often are. Her appetite, her need for rest, and the return of her good humor filled him with a deep satisfaction. She was luminous with a contentment that is only hinted at in the wake of the sexual act. This was the fullest aspect of it and it was he who luxuriated in its warmth. The days before she came to Izeaux faded and were forgotten.

"I was really miserable," she confessed. "I had the most depressing thoughts. I wanted to kill myself and have a gravestone like Dumas's mistress with nothing but four dates, one in each corner: the date I met him, the date we first made love . . ."

It was early summer. The doors to the garden were open.

"As I remember, those were the same dates."

"No."

"I thought it was that memorable night you left the party together."

"Was it that obvious?"

"It was absolutely plain."

"Please," she said.

"I envied you."

He was filled with a sense of well-being. In the light from the windows, late in the day, he thought he looked no more than thirty-five. The clothes in his closet and bureau drawers were always neatly arranged, even the small shining scissors and various bottles on the bathroom shelf. *Le Monde* was on the entrance table with the letters, the bedclothes were fresh, the cook, a woman from the village, was good-natured and calm. His views on politics Catherin disagreed with, he was secretive about money, she would have preferred a younger man, but all in all she felt very disposed toward him, she felt they were bound together in a way that would not be undone. She liked the well-worn surfaces, the comfort of the house. She admired the details of his life.

Of Rand she thought only rarely. She received no letters from him, not even as the birth of her child drew near, but then, of course he did not know where to write.

24

He did the North Face of the Triolet and the *éperon* ridge of the Droites, alone. He could have found a companion, almost anyone would have jumped at the chance, but he left Chamonix by himself and for one reason or another he began climbing that way.

The Triolet is steep, the ice that covers it never melts. It is climbed with crampons, a grid of spikes fastened to the boot. There are two that point straight ahead and can be kicked into the ice. They support the full weight.

He started early. The face was like a huge, descending river, steepening all the way. Its breath was cold. The sound of his crampons was crisp in the silence. He worked methodically, an ice ax in each hand. He became lost in the rhythm. The thought of slipping—he would have shot down the incline as if it were glass—first came to him only when he was far up, and it came in a strange way. He had paused for a moment to rest. The tips of his crampons were driven in a fraction, barely half an inch—that half-inch would not fail. A kind of bliss came over him as he realized this, a feeling of invulnerability unlike anything he had known. It was as if the mountain had ordained him; he did not refuse it.

He was happy, held there by the merest point of steel, above all difficulties somehow, above all fears. This is how it must feel at the end, he thought uneasily, a surge of joy before the final moment. He looked past his feet. The steepness was dazzling. Far above him was a great bulge of ice. There were two ways past it, two ways only.

Each step, each kick into the ice, methodical, sure, took him farther and farther up. He thought of Bray. For a moment it was as if he were there. These lonely faces, these days, were still his, he existed in them. Broken and dead, he was not gone. He had not disappeared, only stepped offstage. The day brought back thoughts of him together with the feeling of triumph as he passed the overhang, the view that awaited at the top.

He was often seen, rope over one shoulder, a pack on his back, headed out. He was off for a stroll, he would say. In the morning he woke among peaks incredibly white against the muted sky. There is something greater than the life of the cities, greater than money and possessions; there is a manhood that can never be taken away. For this, one gives everything.

A strange thing's happened to me, he wrote to Cabot, *I've lost all fear of death. I'm only climbing solo these days. I did the N. Face of the Triolet and the Coutrier on the Verte. Fantastic. I can't explain it. What's happening in the States? What have you been doing?*

It was not only solitude that had changed him but a different understanding. What mattered was to be a part of existence, not to possess it. He still knew the anguish of perilous climbs, but he knew it in another way. It was a tribute; he was willing to pay it. A secret pleasure filled him. He was envious of no one. He was neither arrogant nor shy.

Early in August he arrived at the small refuge hut on the Fourche. It was evening. On the long trek across the glacier he had passed Pointe Lachenal, the Grand Capucin. The sun had passed behind Mont Blanc. He made his way in twilight.

The hut was nearly full. The vast face of Mont Blanc, directly opposite, had sunk into darkness. Voices, when they spoke, were low. Most of the climbers had gone to sleep.

"*Bonsoir*," someone whispered. It was a guide, one of the younger ones. Rand knew him by sight.

"*Bonsoir*."

"*Beau temps, eh?*"

"*Incomparable*."

The guide moved his hand one way and the other—who knew how long it would last—and glanced at the entry Rand had made in the book, "Brenva, eh?"

Rand did not reply.

He made some soup and found a place on the wooden sleeping shelf. As he drew the blanket around him there was a cough in the darkness, the cough of a woman. He turned his head slightly. He could not see her. A sudden loneliness swept over him. He was frightened by its strength. Lying there he fell into dreams. Catherin came to him, just as she was when they first had met. The newness of her dazed him, exactly as then. The little Renault parked behind the shop, the smell of her breath, her sudden smile. How impossible ever to tire of her, her scent, the white of her underclothes, her hair. Her face among the pillows, her naked back, the watery light of mornings in which she gleamed. Her slender hand touching him—he could feel these things, images collapsed in his head. She became a harem, a herd, his mind was wandering, multiplying her as she cried, as she yelped like a cur. The memory overwhelmed him. In the darkness he lay like a stone.

At dawn the sky was overcast. It had begun to snow. No one would climb that day. A few parties had already started down. He noticed the woman who had coughed, he heard her complaining, in fact. She was English, wearing a thick sweater and climbing pants unfastened at the knee. He watched her comb her hair. She turned to him to ask,

"What do you think? Will it clear?"

"Hard to say."

"I can't decide whether or not to go down." Her voice seemed amiable. "How do you manage to stay so calm?"

Rand was boiling water.

"Can I have some tea?" she asked. She watched as he poured it. "Are you really doing the Brenva?"

"Depends."

"And you're going alone." She put in three spoonfuls of sugar. "Isn't that asking for trouble?"

"Not really," he said.

Her eyes were direct and gray. She was English but not like Audrey. She was a different breed.

"But one mistake and it's all over, isn't it?" A pause. "My guide seems to consider you some sort of outlaw," she said.

"Well, guides sleep in warm beds."

"And you?"

"Occasionally," he said.

"I would imagine."

"Are you here for the season?"

"Just a fortnight. I'm with my husband, he's a very good climber, he's been doing it for years. I'm afraid he's a bit irritated at the moment. He's hurt his leg. He fell on the Blaitière, so I came up with a guide but I think I'm a bit over my head.

You're the American who does everything by himself, aren't you? I don't think I know your name."

"Rand."

"Yes, that's it. Rand . . . ?"

"Vernon Rand."

"I saw you come in last night. To be truthful, it frightened me. I wasn't sure I should even be up here. When I saw you, I knew I shouldn't be."

"Well, you have a guide."

He was watching from across the room.

"Even if I had three of them," she said.

Her name was Kay Hammet, she was staying at the Hôtel des Alpes. She left at noon. By then it was snowing harder than before. That night there were only four of them and two went down the next day.

There were plenty of blankets then. He lay bundled up, asleep much of the time, waking to see the snow still falling. The wind made the metal walls creak. There was one other person in the hut. Not a word passed between them.

The storm lasted three days. Afterward, the clouds stayed low, covering the peaks.

On the sixth day, at noon, the door opened and a man walked in, stamping the snow from his feet. It was Remy Giro.

"*Salut*," he said.

"You're the first person to walk through that door in a week."

"I believe it. It's terrible out there. Do you have any soup?"

"No, do you want tea?"

"Anything," Giro said. He watched the stove being lit. "What have you been doing up here?"

"Not a lot."

Giro glanced at the young man sitting at the far end of the hut.

"It was full up when I got here," Rand explained. "It's interesting how they leave, first the guides and clients, then the ones who really didn't want to climb anyway. Then the English, out of food. Finally there's no one left but me and"—he gestured toward the back—"the Phantom."

"Don't you think it would be more comfortable in town?"

"Comfort kills," Rand said offhandedly.

"Have you heard what's happened?"

"No, what?"

"You haven't heard the helicopters?"

"What is it, an accident?"

"Two Italians are trapped on the Dru."

"Where?"

"One is badly hurt."

"That's no surprise. Where on the Dru?"

"The West Face, far up. Above the ninety-meter dihedral. The whole face is solid ice."

They had done two-thirds of the climb and been caught by the storm. They tried everything possible to come down; the ice was too severe. On the second day, realizing they had to do something, they decided to go up again and force the summit. That was when one had fallen. They were somewhat beneath the overhangs.

"They've been there for a week."

"Are they still alive?"

"They were this morning. They've tried everything to reach them. They even lowered a cable from the top but it hung too far out. Now they're trying to go up the North Face and cross over."

"Who is?"

"Everyone. The gendarmes, the mountain troops."

"What about the guides?"

"Yes, of course. The guides."

"They're giving advice."

"No, no. They're trying, too. There are two hundred people involved."

"Why don't they go up the West Face?"

"Ahh," he said.

"Have they tried?"

"I don't think so," Remy said.

"Even the guides?"

"The guides are trying to go up the North Face."

"Of course. Maybe they'll find somebody trapped there," Rand suggested.

"They're trying," Remy defended them.

Rand nodded. He began putting things in his pack. "For five days?"

"It won't last much longer," Remy said calmly.

"Who's this over there? Do you know him?" Rand asked.

"I've seen him in town."

"Can he climb?"

"Probably. Why else would he be here?"

Rand called to him. The young man looked over, unhurriedly.

"Do you want to climb?" Rand asked. In response there was a slight, almost indifferent gesture. "Come on," he said.

25

In Chamonix the effort had reached its final stage. There was little hope. The many attempts of the rescuers only made it more painful, more clear. Calmly, knowingly—for Chamonix knew its mountains—people watched the inevitable. The two Italians still somehow alive on the highest part of the Dru were lost.

It was true they had tried to lower a cable from the top. It had hung a long way out from the face. The conditions were unimaginable. One rescuer had already been killed.

In the streets, walking along and looking for anyone he knew, Rand found a friend of Bray's.

"Do you want to take a crack at it?"

"Don't they have hundreds of people up there?"

"Not where we're going," Rand said.

"I've never been on the Dru." He was a schoolteacher, earnest, somewhat shy. He had very red, almost feverish, lips and coarse hair. His name was Dennis Hart. "All right," he said.

From the army they managed to borrow extra equipment, a radio, even some food. On the way back into town they enlisted another climber, a Frenchman, Paul Cuver.

"We'll be there by seven tonight," Rand told him. "They're giving us a helicopter to the foot of the Dru."

"A helicopter?"

"That's right."

His plan was simple. All other attempts had rejected it out of hand. Rather than seek the most practicable, he would try the most direct way. He didn't know how bad the conditions would be, but he knew the route. They would leave fixed ropes behind to aid in the descent. If they were at the base of the Dru that evening, with luck they might reach the Italians on the second day.

They waited until eight o'clock that night. The helicopter never appeared. Finally, in desperation, they took the train to Montenvers, a special trip was made just before dark. A girl from the hotel kitchen there gave them coffee. They sat on the ground by the doorway. The dining room windows were alight and people were having dinner.

It was after ten when they started down the steel ladders that led to the glacier. The sky was black. They could see nothing above or below. The cold breath of the ice age rose to meet them. By the jerky light of headlamps they began to make their way. Even at night, in the most dismal hours, the glacier creaked slowly. The sound of hidden water came from beneath.

On the far side the uphill path began. The packs were heavy. From time to time someone slipped and fell in the dark. It became colder, whether from the late hour or altitude one could not tell.

At two in the morning they reached the *rognon*. They

crawled into their sleeping bags and lay down wherever they could. The young climber from the refuge hut, Hilm, did not have one. He slept sitting up, leaning against his pack, a worn jacket pulled up over his head.

Daylight woke them. It was after six. There were patches of blue in the sky. The clouds looked thin. The Dru was dark and ominous, dusted with snow. Like a huge organ in a cathedral it seemed capable of deep, chilling tones.

On the lower portion there seemed to be little ice. Higher, it was difficult to tell. The very top, where the roofs were clustered, was hidden by cloud.

"See anything up there?"

Rand had the binoculars.

"No," he said.

"Where are they, exactly?"

"I'm not sure," Rand said.

"There's an awful lot of snow on it."

"Let's have some tea." He was already unpacking the things to prepare it. His eyes burned from lack of sleep. His limbs felt stale. "It doesn't look bad. It looks like it's clearing."

Not long after came the faint, wavering sound of a helicopter. It was far off. Finally they saw it, coming up the valley. It turned toward the Dru.

"Why don't you call them and see what's going on? Something may have happened," Dennis said.

"What do you mean?"

"I don't know. They may have died."

An impenetrable static came over the radio as soon as it was turned on. It was difficult to hear anything. "*Allô, allô,*" Rand called. The helicopter was nearly overhead. "*Les italiens,*" he was repeating, "*comment vont-ils?*"

The helicopter was banking, close to the face. He had the

radio to his ear. There was chatter he could not understand. Then, faintly, "*Ils agitent leurs mains . . .*"

"What did he say?"

"They're waving. They're alive."

"Oh. Good," Dennis muttered.

They were eating bread and jam with dirty fingers, sorting out the gear. Rand and Dennis would lead, the other two were to follow. The couloir looked safe. They'd try it. They descended to the snowfield.

At the base of the mountain, Rand looked up. From here it had lost its shape. Cold as steel, it seemed to rise on and on. Had he really climbed it? Had he climbed it twice?

"Hello, you son of a bitch," he murmured.

It was 7:00 A.M. There were at least twelve remaining hours of daylight. He stood there, taller than the others, almost ungainly, storklike. He was wearing a knit cap under his helmet. Cuver crossed himself with a barely visible gesture. Not bothering to rope up they began to climb.

26

Dennis had been in Chamonix three weeks. It was his first visit. He had never made, here or in England, he had never imagined a climb like this. He could not believe he was doing it. At any moment he expected to be unable to go on. He dared not think about it. Late in the morning as pitch after awesome pitch unrolled, hardly aware of how it was happening he found himself on the most terrifying face.

The climbing was harder than he'd dreamed. The snow had to be cleared from holds. Higher up, there was ice, a slick, unyielding ice that could not be completely chopped away. His hands were cold. He was breathing on his fingers, clenching and unclenching, trying to warm them.

In more than one place he called for the rope, he could not have gotten up otherwise. His helmet was crooked, his gear in disarray. He was on a small cliff, close to the ground, he told himself, it was delicate but there was no risk. If necessary he could jump down, he pretended. He must not let the vastness affect him, if he did he was lost.

Whatever the others felt, he knew they would never reach the stranded climbers. What might happen apart from that, he could not guess. All that allowed him to go on, all that preserved him from panic was a kind of numbness, an absolute concentration on every hold and a faith, complete, unthinking, in the tall figure above.

The clouds were lower. By two in the afternoon it began once more to snow.

"The weather's coming in," was all Rand said.

Dennis waited for something more.

"Shouldn't we go down?" he asked.

"It doesn't look that bad. You've climbed in worse than this."

"Actually, I haven't."

Dennis clung beside him, waiting. The snow was coming sideways, stinging their eyes.

"We can't stay here," Rand said. He looked up to find the way. In his worn clothes and with his unshaven face he appeared to be a secondary figure, someone in the wake of failed campaigns. It did not matter. He would do it. He was not merely making an ascent. He was clinging to the side of this monster. He had his teeth in the great beast.

That evening they bivouacked in the storm. The wind was blowing their matches out. The smallest act took on immense dimensions. They were wet and cold. Cuver sat huddled next to Rand. On the far side of him, half-hidden, was Hilm, the fragment of his profile as impassive, withdrawn, as if they were still on the Fourche. What his thoughts were, Rand could not tell. His own, obsessive, slow, stretched out like an ocean current for endless miles. He was thinking of Cabot and the nights they spent like this.

He was remembering Cabot. There are men who seem destined to always go first, to lead the way. They are confident in life, they are the first to go beyond it. Whatever there is to know, they learn before others. Their very existence gives strength and drives one onward. Love and jealousy were mingled there in the darkness, envy and despair.

From above the snow slid down in airy sheets. None of them slept. They sat silent and close together till dawn, on a narrow ledge, tied to the rock.

The sky grew clearer. In early morning the snow stopped. They climbed all that day, slowly at first and then more quickly, bodies warming, the icy ledge of the night left far behind. In the afternoon the sun came through the clouds. It raised their spirits. They heard the helicopter but did not see it.

Dennis had outclimbed his fear. An exhilaration that was almost dizzying came over him. He was one of them, he was holding his own.

Far above a length of rope was hanging by itself. Rand pointed,

"There they are," he said.

"Where?"

"See it?"

"No, where are you looking?"

"Beneath the overhangs. There. Paul!" he called down. A face looked up. He pointed again, straight up.

"I see it," Dennis cried. "Way up."

"We're not going to reach them today." He cupped his hands to his mouth. "Hello!" he shouted. The sound dissolved in space. There was no answer. "We're coming!" he called. "*Veniamo!*" He paused. "Do you hear them?" he asked.

"No."

"Hello!" he shouted. "Hell-o!" He waited. The vastness of the face was the only reply. As loudly as he could he cried, "We're coming!"

In response, as slow as a dream, something white, a bit of cloth, a handkerchief came floating clear. They had heard him. They were alive.

The clouds were in a layer smooth as water. They had lost their darkness, their density. Beneath them was a band of open sky, a narrow horizon crushed by light.

They called to the Italians from their second bivouac. A head appeared, cautious, almost disinterested. Rand waved. In the morning they would reach them.

27

Tall, weary, a childish grin on his face—such was the image that incredibly rose from the void. The two Italians had been hunched on the narrow ledge for nine days. Nine days of exhaustion, of terrible cold, expecting they would die.

It was the man who was injured, he had broken his shoulder. The girl, who was as ragged as he, had astonishing white teeth. She said something in Italian. Rand couldn't understand it.

"*Parl' italiano?*" she asked.

A little, he indicated.

"*È spaccato*," she said.

"Ah, *spaccato*," Rand repeated uncomprehendingly. Dennis was just below the ledge.

"Come up," Rand told him. "Can you understand Italian?"

"We have company," Dennis said as he reached them.

"What do you mean?"

"Down there. Look."

It was another party, made up of guides. They had crossed

over from the North Face and were now just below. They were calling to him.

Two rescue parties arriving at the same time or nearly—the story reached Chamonix that afternoon. What made it more extraordinary was the discussion that had taken place between them. The guides had come up an easier route and there were seven of them. They wanted to bring the Italians down. No, Rand told them. The helicopter was flying past, there were crowds at Montenvers.

"No," he said. "We got here first. They're ours."

Against the vertical rock in sunlight, motley and at ease, were the four amateurs who had made the rescue—photographs would be in every European paper with the bold reply to the guides, "*Ils sont à nous*." In Chamonix nevertheless was a wonderful mood of satisfaction, as if the reputation of the town had been saved.

That evening they reached a ledge halfway down. The weather had been mild all day. The small stove was burning in the dusk. The worst seemed behind them. A cup half-filled with bouillon passed from hand to hand until it reached the injured man.

"*Molto grazie*," he murmured. He would never forget the courage of his rescuers, he said later, in the hospital. His cheeks were black with a two-week beard. His fiancée was beside him.

"We could not move," she said in Italian. "The ice was everywhere. After Sergio fell, he could not use his arm. We had very little food. The storm went on. We were finished. Then came this beautiful American," she cried.

She was broad-faced, like an Oriental, and had a silky, dark mustache. She was full of passion and life. *Questo bel' Americano* . . . he'd had his picture taken with the others, lounging like fishermen, when they got down to the *rognon*. Then, returning to town, he somehow disappeared. He sneaked in the back door of Sport Giro and into a small office where Remy found him, eating a tangerine. He did not want to talk to any reporters. He wanted the pleasure of being notorious, unknown.

It was not to be so simple. They were looking for him everywhere, the town could not hide him. Remy came back to tell him they were in the front of the shop.

"Look, they're not going to leave you alone."

"Do they know I'm here?"

"The reporters? No, of course not. They came to buy equipment, what do you think?" he said.

Someone was already at the door.

Rand attempted to slip past them, refusing to talk.

They would not leave him alone, he was too singular, too bizarre.

"No," he told them. "No."

"Oh, be decent. It's not we who want to see you," one of them said.

He had always been an actor, the call had never come. Now, in the parking lot in front of the Hôtel des Alpes across the way, he was given his role. He was tired but full of grace. Listening patiently to the questions, he tried to respond. He wore a shy smile, it sometimes grew broader, a smile on top of a smile. His long face loomed on the screens of France, gaunt, natural, the wind blowing his dirty hair. Did he feel himself a hero, they immediately asked?

"A hero," he said, "no, no. It wasn't an act of heroism. It was more a debt I owed the mountain. Anyway, it wasn't me. Four of us did it, I was one of them."

That night they would see him from their dinner tables,

mixed in with cabinet ministers and accidents at sea. Women would watch from kitchen doorways as he looked shyly down at the ground.

This was the mountain he had climbed with Cabot and again with Bray. Bray was dead.

"Yes."

"The great faces exact their price."

"No, not that way," he said. "You pay, yes. You have to give everything, but you don't have to die."

They were watching in old people's homes, in cafés. In the large house in Izeaux, Catherin in her last weeks of waiting saw it. Vigan was at her side. She could feel the child move within her as she watched. She sat quietly. She did not want to reveal the intensity of her interest or the stab of emotion that went with it. She felt faint.

"But John Bray, killed on the Eiger . . ."

Rand was silent. "Yes," he admitted. "I mourn for Bray. Not really for him, for myself."

"By that, you mean . . .?"

Ah, well, he couldn't answer. "He died, but that's not the end of it," was all he could say.

"When you think that the guides of Chamonix," Vigan said, "the gendarmes, the army, all of them . . ." He did not finish the sentence. He rose and stood watching the end.

"You love the mountains . . .," they said.

"Not the mountains," he replied. "No, not the mountains. I love life."

Whoever did not believe him did not have eyes to see. People remembered. It gave him a name. "*Bonjour, monsieur*," the woman greeted him at the *douches*. His honesty had touched them. That worn, angelic face, filled with happiness, stayed in one's thoughts.

That night he had no worries, no concerns. He let his glass be filled and relived the climb. Afterward he slept at Remy's. He slept as he had the first time, long ago, as if all the earth were his own chamber. He slept untroubled, with swollen hands.

When he woke he was famous. His face poured off the presses of France. It was repeated on every kiosk, in the pages of magazines, his interview read on buses by working girls on their way home. Suddenly, into the small rooms and houses, the ordinary streets, he brought a glimpse of something unspoiled. For two hundred years France had held the idea of the noble savage, simple, true. Unexpectedly he had appeared. His image cleansed the air like rain. He was the envoy of a breed one had forgotten, generous, unafraid, with a saintly smile and the vascular system of a marathon runner.

28

In the streets of Paris drivers lowered their windows and called to him. It was phenomenal. His face alone made people turn. Someone would come up to him and in a few minutes there was a crowd. They took him as their own.

"*Mon légionnaire,*" Colette mocked. "How do you like having Paris as your garden?" she said. She was pleased by his fame. She took it as a matter of course. About Catherin she did not inquire. Most likely she knew.

Her apartment was on a top floor near the place des Vosges. People had been invited for drinks—everyone was eager to meet him. Bottles and glasses on the table, the balcony doors open—how beautiful the city seemed, the elegant, worn buildings, the trees, taxis queuing up at the corner, the traffic, the evening light. Her friends were journalists, women, businessmen. They were talkative, well dressed. They had carved out lives.

"How does one climb alone?"

"Alone!" a woman cried. "Is that true?"

"Tell me, what protects you?" someone said.

He saw himself reflected in a mirror on the opposite wall among women's bare arms, the backs of men's heads. The smoke and murmur of conversation rose.

"Nothing actually protects you," he said. The murmur of conversation quieted around him. "It comes from within," he explained. "It's not like gambling. It's not a matter of taking chances." They assumed that a climber is courageous, that like a boxer there is latent in him the strength to kill. "You're prepared for everything," he told them. "If your foot slips you have your hand. You never try something unless you're sure you can do it. It's a question of spirit. You have to feel you'll never come off."

"*Ne pas monter bien haut, peut-être*," a woman recited, "*mais tout seul*."

"What's that?"

"Rostand," she said. She was wearing a silk shirt and ivory necklaces. There was something about these women, poised, calmly wise.

Later, an almost oceanic blue had covered the sky. The television was on. He sat drunkenly on a couch. People were still talking animatedly. Colette was running her finger along one of his.

"Am I going to spend tonight alone?" she asked. She was looking at his hand. Her face was astonishingly young.

Paris and triumph. In his pocket were two thousand francs for the rights to photographs of the rescue. How easily it had come. He remembered music playing, the soft air of night. Her bedroom had thick curtains, chairs, fish barely moving in a greenish, square tank. Her robe was half open. She took his hands.

"You're not too tired?" she asked.

She had a clever face, a face that knew him. Her hair was rich, disorderly, it smelled like almonds. He fell asleep almost immediately, like a vagabond in a barn.

In the morning she picked up a bottle of Evian water from beside the bed and drank. She offered it to him. The bed was large. She slept, smoked, ate apples in it. Her face was naked, her breath a little stale. Her arms were faintly yellow near the armpits, otherwise she might have been thirty.

"You were quite a success last night," she said.

"Was I?"

"Though you wouldn't go to dinner."

"No," he said, "I'm like an animal. I eat when I feel like it, I sleep when I feel like it."

"Yes, I noticed." A stumpy-legged cat with bitten ears was stepping back and forth across them. "*Bonjour, Pilou.*"

So, she would have two animals, she said genially. Despite the disappointment of the first night she was ready to accept him. This was morning; she sat up and combed her hair. The curtains remained closed, the maid opened them at noon.

Colette looked after him, she advised him, sorted out his clothes. He was lazy, basking in the warmth of self-approval without the ability to judge things for himself. An article he had written appeared in the paper. It was absolutely foolish, she said, it was affected, it didn't sound like him.

"What do you mean?"

"You have to be more or less intelligent if you want to give opinions," she said.

"Is that so?"

"Yes, it is."

There were offers to do advertising. He turned them down.

"Now that, you see, is definitely not intelligent," she said.

"After all, there's nothing wrong in it. People like your face, why not let them see it?"

It was against his principles, he said quietly. It was not only against his principles but more, it was something he despised.

"Ah, that." She merely shrugged. "People know you're accepting a little money, they don't care. Nothing could pay you for what you did. The Romans rewarded their heroes," she said. "In Genoa, they were given houses."

"It still doesn't make it right."

"You sold the photos to *Paris Match*," she reminded him.

"They would have been published anyway."

"Perhaps. Look, my darling, in ten years, who will know the difference?"

"And if it's only me?"

She admired him. It was a question he was asking, he wanted her approval. "Yes," she agreed, "that's something. The only trouble, with your habits, you may not be here."

She was the world, he realized, and he an outsider. Moreover, through a friend she could even arrange it so he would be paid more. On the rue de Rivoli she bought him a beautiful jacket of soft leather. She had no particular reason—she felt like it, she said.

He tried it on in front of the mirror.

"Well?" she asked.

The illusion of distant traveler was vanishing. Concession was on his shoulders. "I look like one of your friends."

"Is that bad?"

That night they dined at Lipp. A film star was across the room, annoyed by this unknown rival. At the end of the meal he unexpectedly came to the table and shook hands. His instinct was infallible—every eye in the restaurant was on him. He was making a film at Billancourt.

"Come out and visit me," he said.

September passed. October. The splendor of fall. There is a season of life that lasts forever. Her taste, her telephone, her friends—he adopted all of these. There were nights he felt he'd been dancing too long, he yearned for a simpler life. But it was brief. It went away. The big disheveled bed was his and none other's, the maid who came four times a week, the jacket of glove leather, the kisses on his hands as if he were a priest. He could do anything, he could have anything.

"Would you like to go to Belle Isle?"

"Where's that?"

"It's an island. You take the train from Paris. In the morning you're at the sea."

"It's fabulous," Simone agreed. She was the woman who that first evening had quoted Rostand. "The ocean, the rocks, the air. It's a paradise."

"In November?" he said.

"It's the best time!" they cried.

"Let me go with you," Simone said. "I'll find a place to stay."

Colette made a slight, parental sound with her tongue. "Another time," she commented.

As a friend, Simone accepted this faint cautioning. She understood. They were still talking about the beautiful solitude, the sea, when there was a crash from below. Two cars had collided in the street. Colette went out on the balcony.

"My God!" she cried. Someone had hit her car which was parked in front. "Look at this! Can you believe it?"

She ran downstairs. They watched from above.

"That's so awful," Simone said, staring down. "Is that hers? That one? How could someone do it?" She felt a hand placed near the small of her back. She remained looking down. "I can't understand it," she continued.

Her profile revealed nothing, but the flesh beneath the fabric of her dress had changed: it was unknown but no longer forbidden. Her shoes, her stockings, the weight of her breasts, they were silently being collected. Colette was looking up with a shrug of annoyance, of pleading. She called out something.

"*Quoi?*"

"*On ne peut pas imaginer!*" she cried.

His hand moved slightly, possessively. She seemed unaware. She stood motionless, like a bird in cover. Not a word has passed between them, not a glance.

"A thousand francs, at least," Colette said angrily as she returned, "and the color will never be right. Can you imagine? While we were sitting here!"

Her complaints, her misfortune seemed to isolate her. She didn't want to go to dinner. She was too upset.

"You have to eat. Please, come," Simone said.

"No, that's all right."

"Please."

She failed to notice anything. She stayed behind in the apartment. They went down the stairs. They had barely turned the corner before they embraced.

One woman is like another. Two are like another two. Once you begin there is no end.

29

Women are sensitive, they are shrewd. In the morning there was something strange, perhaps it was a slight sense of distance or even a faint, undetected scent to his skin. Colette watched him sleep. She woke him as she left.

"What time is it?" he muttered.

"Nine o'clock."

He turned over. She was looking at his bare shoulder, the side of his head, in calm appraisal.

"Where did you go last night?"

"Hmm?" He was suddenly wide awake but did not show it.

"Where did you eat?" she said.

"Daru," he yawned. It was a lie.

"Was it pleasant?"

"It was all right," he said.

"I'll call you later."

It seemed somehow threatening. When the front door closed he jumped up and went quickly to the phone. Simone's number was in the address book there. He dialed but there was no answer, she had already gone out. He paced around the apartment, a kind of panic hovering over him. It was a cloudy morning. Traffic sounds rose from the street.

That night they stayed at home. He was uneasy, he tried to seem calm. Whatever she said alarmed him. He knew she was clever, astute. He found himself somehow apprehensive of all that represented her, the apartment, the shop, the comfort surrounding her, the friends with the house on Belle Isle.

Her face looked suddenly older. He could see it clearly, the dryness, the lines around the mouth. He resented her knowledge, her assurance. At the same time, he didn't want to give her up. The evening news was on. The room was filled with a flow of soft French he was barely listening to and the crackle of wood in the fireplace. He must have yawned.

"Tired?"

"A little."

"You can go to bed early tonight," she said.

"I probably will."

"I'm going to Geneva this weekend. Would you like to go?"

"Geneva?"

"You've heard of it?"

"How long will you be gone?"

"Just until Monday."

"I don't think so," he said. "I'll probably stay here."

"You won't be bored?"

"No."

"You're sure?" She was regarding him.

"Yes, I'm sure."

"Um."

"Look," he said unconcernedly, "I think you know this already. I went home with Simone last night."

She admired the coolness of his confession, the brevity. She could not have improved on it herself. "Yes, I know," she said, matching it.

He was slightly thrown off. "I don't believe in hiding things."

She did not reply.

"You're not angry?"

"I'm just curious why you did it."

"I don't know," he admitted.

"You're tired of me already," she said somewhat wistfully.

"No, that's not it," he said.

"It didn't bother you that it might hurt me?"

"Annoy you."

She gave a brief, mirthless smile, "But what is the philosophy behind it?"

"Philosophy?" The word surprised him.

"What is the reason?" she asked. "When someone trusts you, you mean you don't feel any regret if you betray them? Going from woman to woman, from place to place, like a dog in the street, that fulfills you? The hero with such gorgeous ideals, beautiful ideals, you turn your back for a minute and he sleeps with your friend. It's disgusting."

He was silent.

"Say something."

"What?"

"I don't know. Say: Colette, forgive me, you gave me too much, somehow I resented it, I had to do something. Or, Colette, this woman was helpless, foolish, I wanted to find out if she was even the same kind of creature as you, is she really a woman? I thought. Or you could say, Colette, I forgot who I was. I forgot I am really an American, the kind one detests, stupid, ungrateful."

"It's that bad?"

"It's ugly," she said somewhat wearily. "I'm going to bed."

On Friday she went to Geneva, to a comfortable hotel on place Longmalle where she usually stayed. The city seemed fresh, the weather clear. She attended to her business, had dinner, and settled down with new magazines in a smooth, white bed. Unhappy, yes, but she was familiar with it. She knew the medicine for it, she knew it would pass. Further, she knew she would forgive him and they would begin again, much as it was before.

She was wrong.

He had left the apartment and gone to Simone's. He was there only a short time. Simone was nervous, high-strung, she ground her teeth in her sleep. Her pubic hair was harsh.

"You're grinding your teeth." He shook her.

"What?" she said, dazed.

He told her again.

"Why did you wake me up?" she complained. Now she would not be able to go to sleep again.

After Colette, she seemed careful, dull. The sexual attraction did not disappear—she carried that with her despite herself—but it was too much trouble to isolate among all the medicines, real and figurative, that cluttered her life. She was a drama critic for small, Catholic journals. The shelves were piled with books leaning against one another, her table was covered with papers. There was none of the casual comfort of Colette's. These were three rooms where the mind was at work. The only thing she said that made him like her was once, in exhaustion,

"You make love like someone in a novel."

After three days he left.

"Where is he?" Colette asked calmly as they were having a

conciliatory lunch. She had already forgiven Simone. They were like two patients who have had the same illness.

"I found him extraordinary," Simone admitted. "But he also made me nervous. I never really knew what to talk about with him. He's not exactly a polymath. He knows nothing about politics, art, and yet I found myself perfectly willing to believe in him. Whatever it is, he has it despite himself."

"I think it's mainly an ability to look good in old clothes."

"I don't know where he's gone," Simone said. "He was very unsettled. Actually I felt sorry for him. I knew he would leave, it was only a matter of time. His ambition, as far as I can see, is very unclear."

"His ambition?"

"You know him better. Don't you agree?"

"I'm not sure what his ambition is. There's no question, though, where he's going. He knows exactly."

"Where is that?"

"Oblivion," she said. It was not so much a prophecy as a dismissal. She was casting him out of their lives. He would wander elsewhere, exiled, a vanishing figure. "You know, he has a child in Grenoble, a son."

"He's married?"

"No, no. She's one of his many wives. He has greater and lesser wives."

"Original," Simone said dryly though the idea intrigued her.

They were not wives, they were not meant to be wives. They were witnesses. For some reason he trusted only women and for each of them he assumed a somewhat different pose. They were the bearers of his story, scattered throughout the world.

30

He was drifting downward, from the world of cafés and lights to another of dismal streets and long walks home after midnight when the Métro had closed, a city of chance encounters in the company of a strange girl he first saw outside American Express who also had no place of her own. She was blonde, clean-faced, an heiress.

"I think I read about you somewhere," she said.

It was at a party in someone's apartment. A thin-legged dog with a coat of beautiful brown ran ceaselessly from window to window looking out. There was endless striking of matches to light a small pipe.

"Aren't you famous?" she asked. Her name was Susan de Camp. She was sitting across from him. Very matter-of-factly she pulled up her skirt as she spoke and crossed her legs. The pure, narrow white of her underpants was directed straight at him.

In spite of the off-handedness of her life she had a healthy appearance. She was tanned from being in Sicily. Her arms had a golden down. She was scrubbed, alert, casual.

"Where are you staying?" she asked. He was her friend, she'd made up her mind. "Can I trust you?" she said. She had gone to good schools, a brilliant student, in fact. She'd been married to a man in Kenya. "He was fabulous, but he was a drunk. He'd been married at least three times I found out later. You want to go in here?" she asked. "This isn't a bad place."

It was on the corner of rue Verlon. The windows were glazed from the cold. Inside were a number of women, waiting.

"They're always here," she said. "I like to come and watch them. Can you imagine the stories they could tell? I always say hello."

"*Bonsoir*," he greeted them with a sweep of his arm. Several of them replied.

"I told you," she said. "They're my friends. I bet anything they know Gordon." He was her ex-husband—he had been a publisher, a pilot, he owned a coffee plantation. He was still madly in love with her, she confided.

"Where is he now?"

She gave a slight shrug as if bored by the conversation.

"I have some friends near here," she said. "You want to go there?"

That night he lay beside her brooding, more and more discontent, for half an hour, trying to make pleasure finally open its wings.

"That's all right," she said. "Really, I'm used to it."

A sense of disgust and uselessness filled him. The act of love, even disinterestedly or in degradation, is still the most serious act of all. Rather than disappoint her, the failure seemed to bring her closer to him. Perhaps, in fact, she was used to it. Perhaps she even preferred it.

"Really," she confided. "I'm fine."

During January they wandered together. In the stuffiness of endless bars they sat waiting to meet someone or merely waiting. The afternoons were somber. Often it rained. Paris was like a window. On one side there was comfort and well-being, on the other everything was cold and bare, the streets, the cafés, the cheap, ascending smoke. He thought of Chamonix and the clear morning air, standing in the station, the weight of a pack upon him and the solemn, reassuring clank of metal from the bandolier of it hung on his shoulder. Here, hardship was misfortune; there, it was the flavor of life.

Susan sat bundled up in a scarf and a camel hair coat. She was an outcast. She had gone beyond all possible forgiveness of her family, she loved to joke about it, sending them telegrams saying she was so cold she couldn't get out of bed, she was hungry, she was sick.

"Let's go over to the American Library," she suggested, "maybe somebody's there. There's a guy named Eddie who's writing a book on the Middle Ages. Maybe he'll buy us dinner," she said. "I went home with him once."

They walked along the river. There were small fires burning on the *quai*, men sitting beside them. He felt a sense of camaraderie toward them, they were poor, free. He grinned at them, he was at ease.

One of them held out his palm.

"*J'ai rien*," Rand said, almost proudly. He turned his pockets inside out to show them. "*Rien*."

"*La veste*," the man said hoarsely.

"*Oui, la veste*," the others cried.

"They don't believe you. What about your jacket?"

"This? Someone gave me this."

The scornful cries followed them from a distance.

"I don't think you convinced them." Her face was hidden in her collar.

"You don't believe I've lived like that?"

"Oh, I believe it."

"They were drinking," he explained.

That night he looked at himself in the mirror. His face seemed uninteresting. The longer he stared at it, the duller it became.

"What's wrong?"

"Nothing. I'm out of shape."

"You look terrific."

"Do I?" he said. He didn't hate her, she was decent, friendly, it was himself he was tired of. He was tired of following her around, of having her pay for things. He had passed forgiveness also. He could not imagine what he was doing here, what he was waiting for, what he expected to find.

Paris—it was like a great terminal he was already leaving, with a multitude of signs, neon and enamel, repeated again and again as if announcing a performance. The people of Paris with their cigarettes and dogs, the stone roofs and restaurants, green buses, gray walls, he had held their attention for a moment. The *affiches* with his face on them had vanished but he had stayed on. He saw it clearly as, at a certain place in life, one sees both the beginning and end: Paris had discarded him.

31

The sky was flat, the sun a flaw in it. A layer of silence lay above everything. Beneath it, in the streets, sounds were hollow as if in a tin. A winter day in Chamonix, a day when the whiteness eats one's bones.

The Carlton had the look of a building that has been bombed out and only one wing remains. The balconies had iron railings, the windows were faced in stone. The mansard roof was covered with snow which a man was shoveling. He was wearing something attached to his boots—crampons, the points of which, it later turned out, were punching holes in the roof. A voice called up from below,

"Hey, Vern! Vern!"

The shoveling continued. The snow fell in wavering sheets through the air.

"Hey, Rand!"

Hat pulled over his ears and dirty parka patched with tape, he went over to the edge. Someone was waving from the street.

"Who's that?" he called.

"Nick! Nick Banning!"

"Who?"

Banning was a doctor, in his first year of residency, but he looked the same.

"What are you doing up there?" he asked when Rand came down.

"What am I doing? Christ." He was unshaven, his eyes red-rimmed. "What are you doing in Chamonix?"

"I came to see the sights."

"Well, there's Mont Blanc," Rand said.

Banning ignored it. "I read all about you. It was sensational," he said. "I was telling everyone: I know him!"

"It was all right, I guess."

"All right?"

"If you want the truth, it damn near ruined me."

"You look great."

"I know," Rand said caustically.

"It couldn't have ruined you."

Rand took off his hat and rubbed his face with it.

"Believe me," he said.

"You were a hero!"

"I just talked a lot. The French have an expression"—he remembered Colette— "*il faut payer*, you have to pay."

"You're going to have to explain that to me."

"Yeah, well, it would take a while."

Banning had driven from Geneva in a rented car. His pack and sleeping bag were in the backseat. He'd planned to find a place to camp, even in the middle of winter. He had longed to climb these legendary peaks.

"I don't know how much longer I'll be able to do something like this," he confessed.

"With me it's the opposite problem," Rand said.

"Do you know anywhere I could sleep?"

"You can stay with me. There's always room for a friend. Speaking of friends, what do you hear from Cabot?"

"You should have been there when he heard about it. He tried to call you, but you'd gone to Paris."

"Really? Is that true?"

"I haven't seen him for a while," Banning said. "I just haven't had the time. I hear a lot about him."

"Where is he?"

"California."

"I've written to him a few times," Rand admitted. "Not lately."

"He's a strange guy. He's like a searchlight. When he turns your way, he just dazzles you. Afterward, you're left in darkness, you might as well not be alive. Don't misunderstand, I like him. He's in a class by himself. I think he'd do anything for you, but he's absolutely driven. He wants to be first. He wants to be number one. You know that."

"Maybe he will be. Who's he climbing with these days?"

"Various people."

Rand nodded. The conversation was depressing him. The street seemed empty, sound had drained away.

"One thing I'd really like to do," Banning said. "I'd like to take a look at the Dru. Can I get up there this time of year?"

"Not in the snow, " Rand said. "It wouldn't be too easy."

"Where is it?"

"Oh, it's up there. I'll take you to a place where you can see it later." He seemed vague, disinterested in the idea.

Toward evening he was livelier. They went to the Choucas where a photograph of him hung on the wall. He began to tell stories of Paris, sleeping in various beds, being hailed on the boulevards.

"They don't expect me to do anything ordinary anymore, that's the trouble."

"So anyway, what are your plans?"

Rand was silent for a moment.

"Well, don't say anything about this, but there's something I've been thinking about for a long time. In fact, we even talked about it once. The Walker."

"I remember."

"That was before I ever came over here. I'd never even heard of the Dru. The Walker, that was always the big one."

As he was talking, his mind went back to the days when he first had climbed. He was fifteen. He remembered seeing another climber, older, in his twenties, rolled-up sleeves, worn shoes, an image of strength and experience. Now, with absolute clarity, he saw that climber again, his face, his gestures, even the very light. It seemed that in spite of all that had happened in between, the essence, an essence he had seen so vividly in that unknown face still somehow eluded him and he was struggling again, still, to capture it.

"I'm going to do the Walker," he said. He had barely spoken the words before adding, "I'm also going to do the Peuterey." He felt no pride, no pleasure in announcing it. It was somehow flat. "I don't know what I'm going to do."

Banning was listening politely.

"Can you imagine what it would be like to solo the Walker? What kills them is I'm not really that great a climber, I'm not that talented."

"Come on."

"There are lots of them with more talent."

"Not really."

"Lots of them," Rand insisted. The wine had been vanishing, glass after glass. The noise of other conversations rose around their own.

They drove on a snow-covered road. The night was clear. A cold moon illuminated everything, the sky was white around it. Shreds of cloud blew across like smoke. They passed the empty fields of the Biolay. The pines were dark. There was not a house or light. Banning slowed down.

"Are you sure this is the road?" he said.

Rand merely motioned onward. A kilometer farther they came to a barn that was standing by itself. In front of it was a stone trough. Rand broke the crust of ice.

"You want some water?" He was drinking from cupped hands. "Cow water," he added.

He led the way inside into a room meant for storage. It was clean, the floor was of heavy boards. By the light of a lamp, Banning looked around—some clothes, equipment, a shelf of books, a radio.

"The batteries are dead," Rand said. He was lighting the stove. Soon there was a fierce crackling of wood, loud as shots. "It warms up pretty fast," he said.

"How'd you find this place?"

"Oh . . ." Rand shrugged.

"Do you have to pay much?"

"Nothing. Of course, it isn't worth anything."

"Anyway, you're by yourself."

"Yeah, this is the lowest refuge. Capacity: one."

"That's all?"

"At the moment. You want to dry your boots?" He began unlacing his. He sighed. "It's a long struggle."

"In Chamonix?"

"There are times you even think you're ahead. You know,

there was always one thing about Cabot: you're up there together, nothing, just space under both of you, but somehow you're a little farther out than he is, you're risking more."

"How?"

"I don't know. That's just the way it is. You know what I liked about him, the thing I envy most? Carol, his wife."

"I'm getting married next month myself. Hey, what's this?" He had picked up a book.

Rand looked up. He reached for it. "Let me have that," he said. "Do you know anything at all about this guy?"

"Who is it?"

"Mayakovsky. I have to find out more about him." He was flipping through the pages.

"Never heard of him."

"And you're a doctor. Here. Have you ever read his last letter? He wrote it to a girlfriend. You know, he shot himself. *The small boat of love is shattered against the flow of life. I'm through with it. Useless to dredge up the sorrow, the sadness, the . . .*" Here he faltered. "I don't know how to say it, *les torts réciproques . . . Be happy. V. M.*"

Banning had not been impressed with Rand when he first met him. He hadn't known that much about him, he'd even thought him ordinary.

"I didn't know you were interested in poetry."

"Actually I'm interested in very few things, that's the problem," he muttered. "Do you want to know what I'm really interested in? It's disgusting. Making people envious—that's it. That's all it is. I wasn't always that way. There may have been a tendency but not much. I was stronger."

"I envy you," Banning said.

"Don't."

That was what he would remember, those words casually

uttered and Rand lying asleep, as if dead, the snow unmelted on the floor near their boots. In the morning there was light through the ice-glazed windows and the sudden rumble of something outside—Banning jumped up to see what it was. The train to Montenvers was passing not far off. In the daylight the room was even more bare, an inventory of its contents would not fill a dozen lines. Above the shelf there was a postcard pinned. The handwriting was a woman's. The final line he remembered also. *I know you have glory waiting for you*, it read. It was signed with an initial. *C*.

32

There were two reporters waiting by the bridge over the tracks. They followed him across.

What could he tell them? he asked disarmingly—he was taking the train, that was all. One of them snapped pictures as they stood on the platform. There was a crowd. People were turning their heads to look.

Was he going up to the Walker? Was he going to climb it alone?

"You've got all these people wondering what's going on," he said.

"You're carrying a lot of equipment," they noted.

"It's not as heavy as it looks."

"How many kilos?"

"Oh, maybe ten."

"You mean twenty-five," one said.

They talked in a bantering fashion; Rand denied nothing, but admitted very little. Meanwhile a strange metallic pounding hung in the air. He turned to look—it was a workman repairing the rails.

"What are conditions like on the Walker?"

"I'm not really sure. Have you heard?" he asked.

"Ice," one of them said.

"I wouldn't be surprised." He looked again toward the workman. The hammering had a solid quality, unhurried, clear. Iron singing as it entered granite—the thought crossed all their minds.

"Perhaps you should take him with you," they joked.

A light turned red. In the distance, a somewhat ominous rumble. The train was coming.

From Montenvers he descended to the glacier, a lone figure with a pack. There were groups of inexperienced climbers learning to walk on the ice, others heading up in various directions or coming back. Gradually he passed them, passed the Charpoua and the iron ladders fixed to the rock at Les Egralets. By noon he had started up the Leschaux Glacier itself. He was moving steadily, stopping only occasionally to rest.

Afterward they said he had seemed different, it was hard to describe. He was a bit disheveled, perhaps, as if a measure of caring had lessened. His ardor had lost its edge. They expected him to appear at the Leschaux hut, but he didn't go to the Leschaux. He went on alone up the glacier.

He'd been paying no attention to what was ahead, but more and more he could feel it there, a presence in the sky. He could sense it as, from miles away, one feels the sea. He was carrying too much, ice ax, crampons, a sleeping bag, food for five days. Every pound was critical. Still, he needed it all. He had a sketch of the route with every scrap of information he could find, where it crossed the ridge line, where the rock was no good. Finally he stopped and raised his head.

Dark, flanked by snowfields, the greatest pillar of the Grandes Jorasses soared four thousand feet in an almost unbroken line. The bottom was in sunlight. Farther up, it was nearly black.

A human face is always changing but there is a moment when it seems perfect, complete. It has earned its appearance. It is unalterable. So it was with him, that day, as he gazed up. He was thirty—thirty-one if the truth be known—his courage was unbroken. Above him lay the Walker.

There had been good weather, a spell of it, perhaps enough to clear the ridge of ice. From the base, he could not tell, the scale was too vast. He might be early, but the weather would not hold indefinitely. The snowfields didn't seem too large. The rocks at the base looked clean.

He had planned for two nights on the face. About halfway up lay the Gray Tower, the most difficult part. From there, retreat was said to be impossible, the only way off was to continue to the top. He could see no other parties; he was alone. For a moment he felt the chill of desolation but gradually took heart. He began to scramble over easy rocks, not thinking far ahead, emptied soon of everything except the warmth of movement.

It was cold by the time he reached the first ice, which was harder than he expected, even with crampons. He had an intimation that worse was ahead. Carefully he worked his way upward.

In the late afternoon he had reached a vertical wall. The holds were not good. He had managed only a short distance when he decided he could not do it carrying his pack and climbed down and took it off. He tied one end of the rope to it, then started again with the other end fastened to his waist. The rock was slick in places, he didn't trust it. He was climbing poorly, making mistakes. A wind was blowing. It made the face seem even more ominous and bare.

Suddenly his foot slipped off. He caught himself.

"Now, don't get stupid," he muttered. It was not quite aloud. "You can do this. You could do this blindfolded." He looked up. There was a piton. Just get to that. It had been climbed before, he told himself, it had been climbed many times.

"A little farther. . . . There."

He slipped a carabiner in and tied to it. He was breathing hard. More than that, he was chastened. He pulled up his pack.

On top, finally, was a ledge, a good one. He paused to calm himself. It was late. If he went on, he might be caught by darkness. It was better, he decided, to bivouac here.

The stars that night were brilliant. From the ledge he gazed up at them. They were very bright—their brightness might be a warning. It could mean a change of weather. It was cold, but was it that cold? He could not be sure. He felt secure but utterly alone. Within himself, over and over again he was turning the vow to climb this pillar. The higher he went, the icier it would become.

The difficult part lay ahead. In a corner of his mind he was already abandoning the attempt. He could not allow that corner to spread. He tried to stop thinking. He could not.

In the morning it took him nearly an hour to sort out his things. It was very cold. There is a way of climbing dangerous pitches with the rope tied in a large loop and clipped to pitons along the way, but it means going back down to unclip and takes time. He tried this once or twice but found it clumsy and abandoned it.

The rock was now glazed with ice. He had to clear the holds;

even then a thin covering sometimes remained. This part of the Walker the sun did not reach. Several times he slipped. Talking to himself, reciting, cursing, he kept on, stopping to read the route description whenever he could . . . *65 ft. with overhang*. The folds had begun to tear.

He began the overhang. The pack was pulling him backward, off the face. He was afraid, but the mountain does not recognize fear. He hammered in a piton and clipped an *étrier* to it. He waited, letting the venom drain from his blood, and blew on his fingertips stinging from the cold. The Gray Tower was still ahead.

The ice became worse. Things he could have done with ease were dangerous, even paralyzing. Off to the west there were clouds. He was nervous, frightened. He had begun to lose belief in the possibility of going on. The long vertical reaches beneath him were pulling at his feet. Suddenly he saw that he could be killed, that he was only a speck. His chest was empty, he kept swallowing. He was ready to turn back. The rock was implacable; if he lost his concentration, his will, it would not allow him to remain. The wind from yesterday was blowing. He said to himself, come on, Cabot would do this. The kid at the Choucas.

At the foot of the Tower was a difficult traverse. Slight holds, icy footing, the exposure severe. There are times when height isn't bad, when it exhilarates. If you are frightened it is another story.

He was standing with one foot on a small knob. Above was a steep slab with a crack running up it. He began chopping it clean with his ax. He started up. The footholds were off to the side, no more than the rims of faint scars, sometimes only a fraction of an inch deep. He had to clear these, too. His toe kept slipping. The crack had begun to slant, forcing him out on the slab.

There was nothing to hold to. He tried to put in a piton, bits of ice hitting him in the face. There were only ten feet more, but the rock was slick and mercilessly smooth. Beneath, steeply tilted, the slab shot out into space.

His hand searched up and down. Everything was happening too fast, nothing was happening. The ice had weaknesses but he could not find them. His legs began to tremble. The secret one must keep despite everything had begun to spill, he could not prevent it. He was not going to be able to do this. He knew it. The will was draining from him.

He had the resignation of one condemned. He knew the outcome, he no longer cared, he merely wanted it to end. The wind had killed his fingers.

"You can do it," he told himself, "you can do it."

He was clinging to the face. Slowly his head bent forward to rest against it like a child resting against its mother. His eyes closed. "You can do it," he said.

They came up into the meadow to find him. He was sitting in the sunlight in a long-sleeved undershirt and faded pants like a convalescent.

"What turned you back? Was it the weather?"

"No," he answered slowly, as if he might have forgotten. There was nothing to withhold. He waited silently.

"Technical problems . . . ," someone suggested.

He could hear the faint whirring of a camera. The microphone was being held near.

"There was ice up there, but it wasn't that." He looked at one or another of them. A summer breeze was moving the meadow grass. "I didn't prepare," he said, "that was the trouble. I wasn't ready. I lacked the courage."

It was true. Something had gone out of him.

"But turning back takes courage."

He nodded. "Not as much as going on."

"What will you do now? What plans do you have?"

"I don't know, really."

"Will you stay in Chamonix?"

"I'd like to get away for a little rest, I think."

"To the States?"

"Perhaps," he said.

As they were packing to leave, one of the journalists came over to him.

"I don't know if you heard the news. I just heard this morning."

"What news?"

"Your friend, Cabot . . ."

"What about him?"

The air itself seemed to empty.

"He fell."

"Fell? Where?"

"In Wyoming, I think." He turned to someone else. "Wyoming, *n'est-ce pas? Où Cabot est tombé.*"

It was Wyoming.

"The Tetons," Rand said.

"Perhaps. I don't know."

"Yes, sure it was the Tetons. Was he hurt?"

"Yes."

"How bad?"

"I think very."

The blood was slipping from his face. "But he's alive."

A faint shrug.

"You don't know?"

They spoke quickly to one another in French,

"Yes, he's alive."

"How far did he fall?" Rand cried.

"It's not certain. A long way."

33

He had slept all afternoon, or nearly. He was listless, exhausted. The days seemed long.

Toward evening he wrote some letters. He stood on the steps of the post office after it had closed. Faces he recognized passed. He was not sure what he felt, if he was merely nervous and depressed or if the curve of life itself had turned downward. From the outside he seemed unchanged, his face, his clothes, more—his rank. He remained, in the eyes of many, a legend. *Il faut payer*.

Later that night, in a café near the center of town, he saw a familiar face. It was Nicole Vix, alone. She looked older. There were circles beneath her eyes. For a moment she glanced in his direction, their eyes met. It was a shock, like one of those relentless stories where as she goes down in the world he rises and years later they see one another again. He could hardly believe this was the woman for whom he was racked with longing that first, hard winter. She was worn, dispirited. Her moment had passed. He had an impulse to go over to her—she was someone who had been important to him in a way, someone he remembered.

"Hello." She looked up. "Are you still working at the bank?" he asked her.

"*Pardon?*"

"Do you still work at the bank?"

"No," she said, as if she had never seen him before.

"Where are you now?"

"I'm sorry," she said.

"Don't you remember me? It was about three years ago, the winter."

"I'm sorry," she shrugged.

In that instant he tasted a bitterness that was intense.

If he could have left that night, he would have. He had finally turned toward home, his thoughts were all there. Still, they nodded to him as he came along the path from the Biolay in the morning, raised their hands in greeting behind shop windows. He felt like someone who had retired. A strange music—final chords—hung over the town.

On a Sunday he came down the road carrying his things. The lowest field was filled with tourist buses, they were parked in ranks. The people who had come on them had not even wandered off. They were having picnics on card tables. Men in undershirts were lying in the grass, their wives or girlfriends minding children.

At the hotel across from the station were two busloads of Japanese. They were getting out to have lunch at long tables set beneath the trees. All of them were neatly dressed, polite. The women wore sweaters. Many were young.

He stopped among them as if they were children. He was a head taller. He spoke to them in French. At first they did not answer, they were too shy, but his voice and manner were so friendly that soon they began to respond. Would they like a souvenir of Chamonix, he asked? He unfastened his pack and took out his pitons—they were used for climbing, up there, in the mountains, he explained. They were put in the rock.

"Ahh," they said, uncomprehending.

"Here. Like this."

"Ah!" They were giggling, talking. "Weight heavy."

"Very heavy. Take it, it's for you." He was handing them out.

"Oh, thank you. Thank you."

"Where are you from?"

"Kyoto."

"Here, take it. You, too." He was giving it away, the worn steel he had driven into rock that faces blue air. "This one," he said, "was used on the Dru."

They tried to understand him. Ah, yes. The Dru.

34

Catherin stepped from her doorway and into the sunlight. Her car was across the way near a small park surrounded by trees—really not much more than a place where three streets came together. The grass was always tall and untended. Though it faced Vigan's house, was only in fact a few feet away, she had never entered it. She was searching for her keys when she noticed someone sitting in the shade. From the first glance she recognized him. She waited there, her heart racing nervously, as he rose and came toward her. "Hello, Catherin," he said.

He had changed from the last time she had seen him, even from the interviews on television. She could not tell what it was. She greeted him more or less calmly, hardly conscious of what she was saying.

"You look surprised to see me," he said.

"Not really."

"Didn't you get my letter?"

"What letter?"

"I wrote to you, it was at least a week ago."

"I never received it," she said simply.

"That's strange." He waited. "Well, I said I might be coming, that's all."

She began to look for her keys again. Her hand was trembling. He stood there. His letter had not reached her, nor in a sense had he. There was a distance between them, the invisible distance between what we possess and what we will never possess. She was even dressed differently. She was wearing clothes he had never seen before.

"How long have you been here?" she asked, not looking up from her handbag. Vigan had left the house only an hour earlier. The cook had then come. "Did you just arrive?"

"I got here at about eight this morning."

"I see."

"I walked around town for a while . . ."

"I see."

"Not really. What are you looking for?"

"I have them," she said nervously, holding them up. "How did you find the house? Well, you had the address, I suppose."

"It's no secret, is it?"

"No."

"How have you been?" he said.

"Very well. And you? You look a little tired."

"I've been traveling."

"From where?"

"Chamonix."

"Yes, of course."

"How's your baby?" he asked.

"He's fine."

"What did you name him?"

"Jean," she said, pronouncing it as the French do.

"Jean." He repeated it once or twice. "How did you pick Jean?"

"It goes with Vigan," she said.

"Ah. What . . ." He found himself hesitating. "What does he look like?"

"He looks a bit like you."

"Is that right?"

"Yes."

She had nothing for him, he could see that. Nothing remained. She was cool, uninterested. She had already assumed the beauty that belongs to strangers.

"Do you think I could see him?"

She did not reply. Within her was confusion. Further, she was nervous—someone coming along the street might see them standing here. Vigan himself might return. Ever since the baby had come he was more affectionate and unpredictable. He might turn the corner at any moment with a huge bunch of flowers on the seat beside him. And yet, here before her was the lost, unforgotten face of the man who was the father, who would always be.

"Well?"

"I don't think you should have come," was all she could say.

"I had to."

"No, you didn't."

"It was now or never," he said simply.

"What do you mean?"

"I'm going home."

She felt a shock go through her. Even though he had abandoned her, he was now doing more, he was vanishing forever from her world.

"When are you going?"

"Tomorrow. I just came to say good-bye."

"Ah, well. He's asleep," she said. "He's taking his morning nap. Besides, the cook is there."

"I don't want to see the cook."

"Look, it's very difficult."

He said nothing. He had only a mild desire to see his child, it was merely curiosity, but the brevity, the calmness of her refusal was killing him.

"You know, I'm getting married," she said. "Henri is going to adopt him."

"When?"

"In the fall."

"So I may never see him again. This could be the last time."

It was everything, his worn clothes, the faint lines in his forehead, the innocence that clung to him no matter what. He was not weak, he was not begging, he stood there patiently.

"You must promise to go," she said. "You must give me your word."

"Don't worry."

"You promise?"

"You seem nervous about something. What is it? What do you think I'm going to do, steal him? I want to look at him, that's all. Is that so much?"

"Wait here," she said and went inside.

He closed his eyes. When he opened them again, the street was empty. It was not hard to imagine he was elsewhere, in any provincial town, even Chamonix. Behind the walls and fences were small gardens, rows of green laid out in careful mounds. These houses, these villages, except for the antennas on the roofs, were unchanged from a century before. He had come to know this country which was not his own. He felt a sudden overwhelming grief at the thought of leaving it. Something swept over him like a wave. He felt himself—his chest—beginning to crack, to fall apart. He could not help it. He loved her and this love had betrayed him. He stood there trying to withstand things: the houses, people passing, his own worthlessness. He wanted to run, to come back another time with his strength renewed, when he could hurt her somehow instead of suffering this useless longing, this regret.

Above him he heard a sound. He looked up.

The shutters of a window on the second floor had opened and after a moment Catherin appeared. In her arms she held her child. She stood as if alone, calm, unobserved. She was silent, focusing on it all her attention and love. From that distance Rand could barely discern its face. He could see the small hands, the pale hair. After a while Catherin looked down. The infant was moving its arms.

"What?"

She had said something, a silent word Rand could not make out. But she did not repeat it. Instead she drew the child closely to her, hesitated, and stepped back into the room. After a minute her hands reached out to close the shutters.

"Catherin!"

It seemed as if all that had gone before was a journey, that the road had brought him here and ended. He did not know what to do. He stood there. Above him the leaves were sighing faintly, the weight of languorous hours upon them, of endless summer days.

It was in Grenoble on the way north that what she had said finally came to him, like a piece of a puzzle that is turned over and over and suddenly falls into place. He saw it plainly, the long blank wall of the house, the window, the small arms moving aimlessly, one simple word: good-bye.

35

A pale afternoon hung over the sea. It seemed that California was even more crowded, there were more people, more cars. The string of houses stretched farther up the coast. New businesses, signs. At the same time, he recognized it all. It was unchanged. Near Trancas a car slowed down to pick him up. The driver was a heavyset man in a rumpled suit. He'd come straight through from Mexico City, he said, heading for Seattle. He'd only stopped for gas.

"Where are you heading for?" he asked.

"Up to Santa Barbara."

"You should have caught the local. What's your name?"

"Rand."

"Call me Tiger," he said. He was balding, with hair combed long across his scalp. He hand't shaved. "Ever been to Mexico?"

"Yeah."

"I go there all the time. You can have a fabulous time in Mexico. It used to be you could see championship fights for five dollars. That was twenty years ago. Things have changed. When's the last time you were there?"

"Not for a while. I've been in France."

"Is that right?" he said. "Where were you, Paris? I've been to Paris. I used to go there a lot. Are you going back?"

"Maybe. I don't know."

"You want a good address?"

"Okay."

He glanced over, "I mean, really good."

"Sure," Rand said.

"The Louvre!" he said. He burst out laughing and reached into his pocket. "You smoke cigars? Here. Hey, why don't you drive with me to Seattle? Ever been there? I bet you haven't. Great place. That's where I live. Come on. My wife will cook us a tremendous dinner. Her name's Galena, how do you like that? She's Russian. She's a goddess, a real goddess. They have an expression for women like her. You know what it is?"

"No."

"Heavy hitter. You like that? That's what she is."

He dropped Rand off on the highway at Santa Barbara.

"See you around," he said. He sped off.

The day was warm. The sea horizon shimmered. Birds were singing as he walked uphill.

The house was a white Victorian or at least influenced by the period. It was low, only one story high, and set back from the street.

He rang the bell. There was a sound of footsteps, a pause, and Carol opened the door. She was in a shirt and pants. Her face was bare as if she had just gotten up or washed.

"Rand!" she cried. She embraced him. "I'm so glad to see you. You look wonderful. Did you just get in?"

"This morning," he said. "How are you?"

"Not bad. Really not bad. We've had wonderful weather. Come on in."

He followed her into the hall.

"Nice house."

"It's very nice. Wait till you see the garden. Just leave your things there. Let's go in back."

She led the way through the kitchen and opened the screen door. There was a porch and two wooden steps.

"Darling," she said, "look who's here."

A man was seated by a glass table in the shade of the trees. He turned his head. He was wearing a blue sport shirt with a bamboo pattern and short sleeves. His arms were powerful. He raised one.

"Hello, you bastard," he said. It was Cabot. He was sitting in a wheelchair. He turned himself around and extended his hand. "I thought it was time you appeared."

"Same old Jack. How've you been?" Rand asked.

"What a question."

"You look fine."

"Oh, don't mind all this," Cabot indicated. "You'll get used to it. When did you get in? How long can you stay? We've got a room for you, did Carol show it to you?"

"Not yet," she said.

"It's the best room in the house. It's the room I'm going to die in. Come on"—he started off in his wheelchair—"follow me, as they say."

He was paralyzed from the waist down, his legs in the limp cloth of a cripple's pants. The fall had almost killed him; he had been in a coma for a week. At first they thought he would never come out of it and only half of him did. For days he lay while they conducted tests and treated him. Meanwhile he was engaged in a secret, a crucial effort of his own, he was trying by any means, even by force of will alone, to make some movement with his toes. He could almost see them do it but they never did. He would start again and continue until he was exhausted, lie quietly for a while and begin once more. He had no pain, no feeling, nothing at all. His legs might have belonged to someone else.

"His spine was broken," Carol explained later. "The nerves don't regenerate. I guess you know that. Almost any other nerve they can patch together, but this one they can't."

"Why is that?"

"The doctor explains it by saying it's like a Transatlantic cable that's been cut. Those thousands of tiny strands, it's impossible to match them up again."

"And that's it?"

"I'm afraid. He'll never get out of his chair."

"What else does it affect? Any inner organs?"

"Everything below the waist," she said.

Outside birds were singing in the full heat of afternoon. The sound seemed to cover the house. Rand felt drowsy. Looking out at the haze-covered hills, he felt he had come to a kind of hospital himself, that he had an illness they would not yet divulge.

That evening Cabot's lawyer dropped by. She was a woman, no older than Rand, aggressive, confident. Her name was Evelyn Kern.

"Glad to meet you," she said. "I've heard so much about you."

They were filing a suit against the insurance company. The settlement after the accident had been small.

"We have to get him some money to live on," she explained, "not to mention medical expenses."

It was very easygoing and casual. They sat and drank. They talked about the past.

"I hear you tried the Walker," Cabot said.

"That's about all you can say—I tried."

"What happened?"

Rand shrugged.

"Your glass is empty. Carol, get him a drink, will you? How high did you get?"

"I could have gone higher."

"A lot higher, as they used to say."

"What is the Walker?" Evelyn asked.

"It's part of the Grandes Jorasses, a ridge that goes straight up."

"It sounds terrifying."

"It's a classic. I always wanted to do the Walker," Cabot remarked.

"Maybe you will," Rand said.

There was an awkward silence.

"You going to carry me up that, too?"

"Who knows?"

So began his visit. The garden was filled with pines and a pair of huge palms. Past the back fence was cane grass, tall and rustling. Carol often worked outside, weeding and watering the plants. She knelt on the ground, the long nape of her neck bent forward, bare. Her legs were lean and tanned. She turned and sat back, aware of Rand's presence.

"This is my green tent," she explained. The branches met over her head. Sunlight filtered through.

On the other side of the hedge a neighbor, Mrs. Dabney, was watering. She was in her sixties. She had a kerchief over her head and wore a halter which gave glimpses of ruined flesh. Her husband had had two heart attacks.

Rand sat sunning himself on the steps, shirtless.

"You're going to frighten her," Carol warned.

"Frighten her?" Mrs. Dabney was keeping up a spray of

water on her jade trees to show she was occupied. "She comes a little closer every day." He raised his voice, "Those are beautiful hibiscus, Mrs. Dabney."

"They're the state tree of Hawaii," she answered, "did you know that?"

"No, I didn't."

"We were just there for a two-week visit," she said. "My husband and I."

"Is that right?"

"We went to all the islands," she said with a friendly smile.

Blue Pacific days. In the morning, mist and the sound of birds. The dark, shadowy fronds plunged down from the heights of the palms. Carol's footsteps in the hallway. Sometimes, lying in his room, Rand imagined they were lingering.

He knew she was watching him. He could feel her glance in the kitchen or at the table. At times, without deliberation, their eyes would meet—she would not look away. He had always admired her. She was returning this admiration.

Cabot drank. He had two or three before dinner and then wine, he couldn't sleep otherwise. If he came to the surface in the predawn hours the same thoughts kept passing through his mind. The wheelchair with its chrome glinted in the moonlight near his bed.

He had never slept well, even before the accident. In those days when he woke he would dress in darkness and go out and walk. Sometimes he was gone for hours. When dawn came he would be on the highest point around, watching the sky lighten and then turning homeward.

That had been taken from him. He lay now staring into the dark. He'd prayed to God, he'd read poetry, philosophy, trying to force his life into a new shape. During the day it seemed to work but at night it was different, it all leaked away and he was a boy again imagining the world and what he would do in it, except that his legs lay limp as rags.

He raised himself on his elbow. One at a time, he lifted his legs to the floor. He pulled the wheelchair close and lowered himself into it. Silently he went down the hall.

"Vern?" He pushed open the door. "Are you awake?"

"No."

"Talk to me."

"What's wrong?"

"I can't sleep."

Rand fumbled with the light.

"If I have a couple of drinks I'm usually all right, but tonight I just couldn't sleep. It's funny, I used to watch my father pouring it down. I had nothing but contempt for him in those days. Some nights he couldn't even talk."

"What time is it?" Rand asked.

"About three."

"Come on in."

"You don't mind?"

"No." He sat up. "No, I've been wanting to talk."

Cabot grinned. "You? Talk?"

"I'd like to find out what really is wrong," Rand said.

"What's wrong? I'm a lousy cripple."

"Is that true?"

Cabot stared at him.

"I've been watching you. You're sitting there reading. Evelyn comes by, you have a few drinks. You're taking it pretty calmly."

"That's what you think."

"Carol is, too."

"You just don't know," Cabot said.

"What do you mean?"

"You don't have any idea. I'm not calm. I'm just waiting."

"Waiting for what?"

"The truth is, I was planning to shoot myself. I told that to someone at the hospital, another paraplegic. I thought I was going to show him how a man behaves or some damn thing. All he said was, make sure you don't miss and paralyze your arms."

"How is it you still have strength in your arms?"

"Didn't Carol explain it to you?"

"She tried to."

"My arms . . . are good . . . " He reached over for Rand's hand. He began to press it to one side, his other hand holding a wheel of the chair. They struggled against one another. The sinews of his neck stood out; slowly he was forcing Rand's arm down. Finally he released it. He was breathing hard. "It's down here I'm a little weak," he said.

"I was going to ask about that."

Cabot said nothing. He seemed almost disinterested.

"What exactly do you have left?"

"Below the waist, nothing."

"Nothing?"

"Absolutely zero," Cabot said amiably.

"I was right. You're taking it calmly."

"Well, you try it."

"And your wife is, too."

"She hasn't got much choice."

"There's always a choice."

"She hasn't left yet, if that's what you mean."

"Oh, she's not going to leave . . ."

"I'm glad to hear that."

". . . not as long as you're in a wheelchair."

"What makes you so sure?"

Rand shrugged.

"Because I'm not," Cabot said.

"She wouldn't leave a cripple."

"You think that's what's keeping her here?"

"Ah, Jack, I don't care about that. I'm thinking about something else. You know the first thing I heard was that you were probably going to die. But you didn't, you fought your way back. Then I hear that you're crippled . . ."

"Go on."

"Do I believe that?"

"That's not really the question," Cabot said quietly. "The question is: Can *I* somehow believe it?"

Until morning, when the pale green tendrils of Mrs. Dabney's star pine waved dreamily as if beneath the sea, they talked, their voices sometimes raised in argument but more often quiet, confiding. There was an understanding between them, the kind that has its roots at the very source of life. There were days they would always remember: immense, heartbreaking effort and at the top, what rapture, they had shaken each other's hand with glowing faces, their very being confirmed.

36

Carol had gone for the evening. The house was still, it was the chance Rand had been waiting for. He sauntered into the room and sat down.

"Evelyn was here earlier. You missed her," Cabot said. He was watching the evening news as usual, a glass in his hand.

"What did she have to say?"

"Oh, legal stuff. She wanted to talk about you. She's very interested in you."

Rand had gotten up and was pouring himself a drink.

"It probably doesn't surprise you," Cabot said.

"No."

"I don't know what you said to her. You told her something about climbing . . ."

"Too much," Rand commented.

"Anyway, it floored her."

The hour was tranquil. In the dusk a bat flew recklessly

above the dark pines, changing direction like a bird that has just been hit.

"I decided to see if I could shock her," Rand admitted. "So I told her the truth."

"Such as?"

"I told her I'd been climbing for fifteen years. For most of that, ten years anyway, it was the most important thing in my life. It was the only thing. I sacrificed everything to it. Do you know the one thing I learned about climbing? The one single thing?"

"What?"

"It is of no importance whatsoever."

"Is that what you told her?"

"Whatsoever," he said.

"What is?"

"You know as well as I do: the real struggle comes afterward."

Sometimes when they talked it seemed as if they had arranged themselves casually—Cabot had merely sat down in a wheelchair that happened to be there. It was as if he might stand up at any moment, discarding his incapacity like throwing off a blanket. Sometimes he actually seemed on the very point of rising and then, as if warned, he relented. Rand had noticed this. It was difficult to know what convinced him, perhaps something hidden. Truth lay beneath the surface.

The California night was falling, the ocean darkness. Another day had passed. He sipped his drink and reflected quietly.

"Something's happened to us, Jack."

"Has it? I hadn't noticed."

"It's happened to me, too. I'll tell you something I bet you're going to try and deny."

"What?"

"You're being betrayed."

"Ah, that."

"I mean it."

"We never are but by ourselves betrayed . . . ," Cabot recited.

"That's only half of it. Do you want to know the rest?"

There was a silence. Cabot waited.

"The people who claim to be helping you, Carol, Evelyn, the doctors, they want to keep you in that chair."

"Oh, have another drink."

"I mean it." He was silent for a moment. "You know, I always believed in you, I did from the first."

"So?"

"In your strength, desire. Your will to succeed."

Cabot made some vague reply.

"I still believe in you."

"What are you getting at?"

"You've surrendered. I've seen you though, when you weren't aware of it, start to stand up."

"It's a reflex."

"I know you can do it," Rand said.

Cabot wheeled himself to the table near the door to turn on the lights.

"I know you can do it, but you're not going to. You've given up." He was speaking to Cabot's back. "And if you've given up, where does that leave me?"

"You?"

Rand waited.

"I don't know," Cabot admitted. He was filling his glass. "I know where it leaves me. I'm not a victim of hysteria or some destructive urge. I know you think that, but there are such things as physical problems. No amount of belief can overcome them. I mean, death is an example. Do you believe in death?"

"I don't know."

"Well, I do."

"But you're not dead."

"No."

There was a dedication in Rand's voice, a seriousness that would not be put aside by indifference or drink. He was trying to force out the truth or some form of it, difficult because truth was reluctant and could alter its appearance. It was one thing in the high reaches of the Alps. It was another in a house in Montecito lighted against the darkness where Cabot was sitting on a rubber cushion in a gleaming chromium chair with something twisted in him, some crucial part that could not be touched.

"You were always ahead of me," Rand said. "I'd never have gone to Europe except for you."

"You might have."

"Do you remember the nights we camped at the foot of the Dru?"

". . . unfailingly bringing rain."

"You gave me all that. You made me do the greatest things of my life."

Cabot didn't know what to say. "It's funny, isn't it?" was all he could manage.

"Now you just have to do one more thing . . ."

"You know, you're like my aunt. She says if I only pray, if I pray hard enough, then who knows what will happen? She won't stop telling me that, she'll never stop believing it. She's a nice woman, I've always liked her, but she's not a doctor. God's a doctor, I know, but Auntie, listen to me, even God can't make me walk. I've tried. I really have tried." He looked at Rand openly. He was too proud to beg but he was asking for understanding. "Believe me," he said.

"I've talked to your doctor."

"Oh, yeah?"

"He told me something I can't understand: that there's nothing physically wrong with you. Something is keeping you in that chair."

Cabot in the confusion of drunkenness was hearing things he knew were untrue. They seemed to swim crazily, daring him to refute them.

"All right, something's keeping me in this chair," he said warily.

"What is it?"

"I don't know."

"Have you lost your courage? Like me?" Rand said.

"I don't think so."

"Can you prove it?" Rand said. He poured his glass half-full like an adversary prepared to spend the night and at the same time raised his hand from between his legs. In it, cool and heavy, was a pistol.

Cabot stared at it. "That's mine," he remarked.

"There's a bullet in it. You don't have to do anything I don't do."

A car turning up the driveway, Mrs. Dabney at the back door, the telephone ringing, Cabot was waiting for a summons back to reality.

"If you've lost your courage, you've lost everything. It doesn't matter after that." Rand drank. "I'll go first."

Cabot suddenly reached for the gun.

"Don't," Rand said, holding it away from him. He cocked it and spun the cylinder. "The leader never falls."

Cabot watched him put the muzzle almost carelessly next to his temple and pull the trigger. There was an empty click.

"Your turn."

"No."

Rand said nothing.

"I can't," Cabot said.

"Have a drink."

"I've had enough."

"You've already died," Rand said.

"Not quite."

"I was with you. We were caught up there. Lightning was hitting the peak. You're not going to back down now?"

"I'm not drunk enough."

"Go ahead," Rand commanded.

Cabot stared at the gun. Its darkness was intense. It was radiating power. He picked it up. He put it to his head. Slowly he pulled the trigger. Click. The hammer fell on an empty chamber. A sudden rush of happiness, almost bliss, swept over him. Rand reached for the gun.

"Climbing," he said. He raised it to his head once more. Another click. "Come on up."

The bullet was in one of the remaining chambers. The gun came to his hand like a card in a poker game, Cabot barely looked at it. He was staring at Rand. He had a sense of dizziness as the blunt, heavy muzzle touched near his eye, an eye that would not even, he thought clumsily, have time to blink. It was going to end like this. He resisted it, he tried not to believe it even as he knew it was true. The end, which was impossible, which was never going to come. His face was wet. His heart was beating wildly. His face showed utter calm. He squeezed the trigger.

Click.

"Now we're getting somewhere," Rand said.

"That's enough."

Rand had hold of the barrel.

"We've come this far." His eyes were burning, his concentration was intense. "One more."

He raised the gun. Cabot reached forward to stop him. A glass went over and crashed to the floor. Almost in the wake of it, concealed, the hammer fell.

Silence. Cabot took the gun.

"That's it," he said.

"No."

They stared at one another.

"I can't."

"One more."

He closed his eyes. The room was spinning.

"You have to," he heard.

The lights of the world would go out, the night devour him, he would be at peace. He was this close. His thoughts were tumbling, pouring past. He was clinging to the final moments.

"Pull."

He started to.

"Pull!"

His finger tightened.

"Pull!" Rand urged.

The hammer fell. A click.

He hardly knew what was happening. Rand had leaped to his feet.

"You did it!" he was shouting. "You did it! Now get up! Get up!" Suddenly he grew calmer. "You can do it," he pledged. "You can! Get up!"

He began to shake the wheelchair. Cabot's head was bobbing. They were like drunken students breaking furniture. Belief was flooding the room.

"You can! You can!"

Across the narrow path between the houses, Mrs. Dabney sitting with her bathrobe-clad husband could hear the shouting.

A violent force was pulling at the wheelchair, tilting it, spilling Cabot to the floor where he sat in a heap, legs bent curiously, and began to laugh.

"Walk to me!"

Cabot was laughing.

"Walk to me! Jack, you did it. You can walk!"

Cabot tried to catch his breath. The room was spinning around. "Oh, God," he was pleading helplessly, "please." It took him a moment to realize he was alone.

"Vern?"

He heard nothing. He called, dragging himself toward the door, "Vern."

The hallway was empty. From the back room came a faint sound. Even if he had never heard it before, it was unmistakable, the sound of cartridges being inserted.

"Vern!" he called.

Rand came out, his hand at his side. He seemed strangely calm. "This works now," he said.

Cabot's glance fell for a second to the gun.

"Look at you. Your chair's on its side, you're sitting there. You can't even get up."

"I can get up," Cabot said.

"You're useless. We're both useless," he said. "The only question is who should shoot who?"

He seemed completely dispirited. Cabot felt a sudden, deep sympathy toward him—he did not know why it was so overwhelming.

"Jack . . . " he heard.

"Yes?"

He looked up. The gun was raised.

"I'm going to count to ten. If you don't get up and walk toward me, I'm going to pull the trigger, I swear that before God. Because you're not a cripple. I know that."

"I know what you're trying to do."

"One."

"I didn't know there was no bullet in it," he said. "You weren't risking anything, but I was."

"Two."

"Oh, hell," Cabot said, abandoning the struggle. He turned his head, not even looking up. He'd had enough of it.

"Three."

Cabot waited stoically.

"Four." Rand was holding the gun in both hands, steadying it.

"I can't walk," Cabot said angrily.

"Five."

"Jesus Christ, I can't even piss."

"Six."

"Go ahead, shoot," he said.

"Seven. Get up, Jack. Please."

Cabot raised his eyes. As if the idea were his own, he put his palms on the floor. He began to try and stand.

"Eight. Get up."

With the strength of his upper body, which was considerable, he was trying—like an animal in the road dragging its hindquarters—he was struggling to somehow get to his feet. His face was wet. The veins stood out in his forehead.

"Nine."

He did not hear it. Everything in him was concentrated on the effort.

"Ten," Rand said.

A deafening explosion. Cabot fell. Another, the sound was immense in the closeness of the hall. The second shot, like the first, made a hole in the wall behind Cabot's head. He was lying, cheek pressed to the floor. Rand fired again. Once more.

Carol came home toward midnight. She'd been at a friend's. She found her husband on the couch, his shirt dirty, hair disheveled. The wheelchair sat empty.

"What is it? What happened?"

He was watching the television. The room was in complete disorder.

"Nothing," he said. "It's all over. I thought you were coming home at eleven."

"I lost track of the time. What have you been doing?"

"Nothing, really. Rand fired some shots."

"Shots?"

"Mrs. Dabney got excited and called the police."

"He fired shots at what? Where is he?"

"He's gone," Cabot said. "I guess he'll be back. He borrowed the car."

Just then she noticed the bullet strikes.

"My God," she said. "What are those?"

"Holes," he said.

37

"Louise?"

"Yes," a sleepy voice said, "who's this?"

"You don't know?"

There was a pause.

"Rand? Is that you?" she said. "Where are you?"

"I see you haven't forgotten my voice anyway."

"What time is it?"

"It's about seven-thirty."

"You always did get up early. Where are you? Are you in town?"

"No."

"Where?"

"Oh, I'm up north here. How've you been?"

"Pretty good. And you?"

"How's Lane?"

"I'll tell you when I see you. He's been in trouble."

"What kind of trouble?"

"I'd rather not talk about it on the phone."

"That's too bad. Is he there?"

"He spent the night at a friend's. Where, up north?"

He looked around.

"Oh, I don't know," he said. "I'm in some gas station."

"When did you get back?"

"A few days ago."

"Well, come on down."

"I will," he said. "I wish I were there right now."

"Well, why aren't you?"

"I had some things to do." He'd wanted to talk to her, but now he did not feel like it. There was really nothing to say. "You know those boxes of mine?"

"Yes, What about them?"

"There's a good fishing rod in one of them."

"A fishing rod?"

"Lane might like it."

"Are you all right?" she asked. "You sound a little strange."

"Do I? No, I'm all right."

"I got your letter," she said.

Farther down the road there was a bridge beneath which a small stream was flowing. He walked down the embankment and washed his face. The sun was coming up behind the hills. There were empty beer cans in the water.

He drove with a lazy contentment, his thoughts drifting. The invincible country floated past. He was seeing things with a fantastic slowness, faces in windshields, names of towns. He was thinking of his father and going hunting as a boy. They had an old twenty-gauge and a handful of shells. The wind was blowing across the fields. Far off they could see the huge, wavering flocks heading south. They had no decoys. A man came along and told them they'd never get any geese that way. They had no license either.

A whole life seems to pass on the road. The sun shifts from one window to another, houses, cities, farms rise and disappear. In a field near Shandon he saw a dead colt, the mare standing alongside it, motionless, leaning slightly. The colt seemed shrunken as if melting into the earth.

He remembered the year they drove from Indiana with a bag of hard-boiled eggs and nothing else. His dog wouldn't eat eggs, they had no extra money for food. They parked by a river in Utah in the evening. Clouds of insects rose. The current slid by, green and silver. In Elko they drove up a bumpy road to a kennel next to—he would never forget its name—the Marvin Motel.

"We'll be back for him in a couple of days," his father told the man.

The dog was sitting behind the wire fence, his white chest showing, watching them drive away.

He thought of Cabot. The mountain had been covered with snow when they were coming down. They had abseiled down the ridge. It was cold, especially lower down when they passed through waterfalls. Cabot was strong, stronger than he was by then. They came down as fast as they could, it was riskier than the climb.

He turned east near Volta and crossed the valley. By then it was afternoon. He was not, he said to himself, a short-term soldier. The hands on the wheel were veteran's hands. His heart was a loyal heart. There is a length to things determined by hidden law. To understand this, to accept it, is to acquire the wisdom of beasts. He was a veteran, a leader, but his pack was scattered, gone. Behind him was a California where wave after wave of migrants had come to rest. They had bought houses, worked, run stores. Behind were refineries, suburbs, empty bottles in the streets. Ahead was the final refuge.

The road was empty, it seemed to drink him, to lead him forth. The late sun was flooding the land. In the rearview mirror it was brilliant, like a shot. One white horse was standing in the fields alone, no sky, no earth, like a print.

He saw himself in the mirror, past the life of which he was the purest exemplar, which he thought would never spoil. He was suddenly too old. His face was one he once would have scorned. He was facing winter now, without a coat, without a place to rest.

That evening he came to a town, Lakeville. Dirt sidewalks, frame houses, yards stacked with firewood. The supermarket had its lights on. On a hill was an abandoned church. Enormous trees. Quiet, cool air. Near the outskirts was a corrugated-iron warehouse. Kids were playing softball near the trailer park. He sat there on an old engine block. The evening was silver and calm. He had meant to drive farther but he could not. Something had gone wrong. He was almost in tears.

He had gone as far as he could, had climbed as high. He could go no farther. He knew what was happening, his knees were beginning to tremble, he was coming off. At that moment he did not want to slip, still grasping desperately for a hold, but instead to suddenly jump clear, to fall like a saint, arms outstretched, face to the sky.

He thought of dying. He longed for it. His world had come apart. He wanted to have everything, every animal, insect, the snails on the garden path, girls with their suntanned shoulders, airliners glinting in air, all, to cease their clamor and resume at last the harmony he had the right to expect. He had no fear of dying, there was no such thing, there was only changing form, entering the legend he was already part of.

He lay all night on the ground, facedown, exhausted. Early in the morning he headed north. He was going up into the mountains, the Sierras.

There were many stories. A climber was seen alone, high up on Half Dome or camping by himself in the silent meadows above Yosemite. He was seen one summer in Baja California and again at Tahquitz. For several years there was someone resembling him in Morrison, Colorado—tall, elusive, living in a cabin a few miles outside of town. But after a while he, too, moved on.

Cabot always expected a card or letter. It would be slow in coming, he knew, but eventually he would hear something. For a long time he believed that one way or another Rand would reappear. As the years passed, it became less and less sure.

They talked of him, however, which was what he had always wanted. The acts themselves are surpassed but the singular figure lives on. The day finally came when they realized they would never know for certain. Rand had somehow succeeded. He had found the great river. He was gone.

38

It was a gray day. The clouds were low and level as the land. The gulf was flat. Birds were sitting on it. From time to time the surface of the water broke and scattered—jack were feeding beneath. The neon sign was unlit at Ruth's. Outside a few cars were parked.

"Watch it! Watch the run!" Bonney cried. "Ah, hell."

"Right up the middle," the bartender said.

"They're killing us. All right, give 'em the field goal."

"What is it, thirty yards?"

They were silent, watching the preparations.

"Now block it!" Bonney called out.

"The kick is up . . . it's . . . no good! No good, off to the right!" the announcer said. The crowd was roaring.

"All right!" Bonney cried.

Ruth's was on the highway just at the edge of town. It was a Mexican restaurant at night.

The screen door slammed. Bonney's brother came in. "Hey,

where've you been?" Bonney said. "I thought you were going to watch the game."

"I fell asleep. You know what happened? Some woman woke me up at eight this morning."

"Some woman?"

"Yeah, she was real sorry, she said. She could tell I was asleep. I said, who is this? You know what she said? It's your mother, she said. I said, lady, my mother's been dead for three years."

"Who was it?"

"How should I know? What's the score?"

"Twenty to three."

"Favor who?"

"Dallas."

"I'm dead! What period?"

"Third quarter," Bonney lied. "You already missed most of the game."

"The third quarter? Already?" Dale Bonney pulled up a stool and sat down. He was younger than his brother, not yet thirty. He didn't look like him, he was shorter and his hair was nearly gone. The brothers were inseparable. "Give us a beer," he said. "You make any bets?"

"Did you?"

Dale nodded.

"How many points did you get?"

"Six."

"Six? Forget it," Ken Bonney said.

The blue team was moving now. One of their backs had gone thirteen yards.

"Who was that? Was that Hearn?" Ken said. "Is that who it was?"

"I think so," the bartender said. "No, it was Brockman."

"Brocklin."

"Is this really the third quarter?"

There was another run and a fumble.

"Oh, for God's sake!" Ken cried. The runner was hurt, he was lying on his back. "*That's* Hearn!" he said as if he'd suspected it. "Get him out of there! Hearn, you're through! Put in somebody younger!" The player was being led slowly off the field. Ken turned away from the bar. He made a helpless gesture to the only other customer sitting at one of the tables. "Would you bet on a team like this?" he asked.

The man looked up. "Which one?" he said.

"Hearn! What are they thinking of? They *want* to lose."

There was a pause.

"Go on," the man said.

"I give up, that's what."

"You know a lot about it, eh?" There was something too calm, almost indifferent in the voice.

A faint warning, the glint of danger, reached Bonney. He turned away. The door banged. A woman came in wearing soft crepe slacks and high heels. "Hi, Paula," he said.

"Hi, Ken." She sat down with the man at the table. "Sorry I'm late," she said.

"How's Fraser?" Ken called from the bar.

"He's fine. He's in Atlanta."

"What's he doing there?"

"He's living there," she said. Then, across the table, "Have you been here long?"

"Forty-two minutes."

"God, can't you be exact? Who's playing?" she asked.

"I don't know. Dallas and somebody," he said.

Paula Gerard was a teacher. She was divorced. Actually, she admitted, she'd never been married, she just took his name.

She had dark hair and a quick, carefree smile. She always seemed a little untidy, perhaps it was her clothes. She told outrageous stories, especially when she was drinking. She swore they were true.

She'd been divorced for almost a year. Fraser was a businessman. He never really worked. He played tennis, drank, and spent his family's money. He was really very funny, she said. Once they flew to London and on the immigration card under "Sex" he wrote, yes, a lot. But he was spoiled and weak. She'd put up with him for years. She'd done things she never thought she'd do, she said.

Bonney watched them drive away. "Who was that?"

"Some guy, I don't know his name. She's been going with him for a while."

"What is he, a little crazy?"

"Could be," the bartender replied.

The afternoon was fading. Throughout the east, in the ominous quiet that surrounds stadiums, the final quarter was being played.

They drove along the sea which was metallic, smooth. The signs of motels and roadside restaurants were on. He seemed moody—that was often so. She used to blame it on his working alone; he ran a wrecking yard for a man in Pensacola, it was over toward the bay. A car would be brought in crushed almost double, doors jammed, the seats glittering with broken glass. "Have to be some drunk to live through that," the tow-truck driver would say.

He liked it, the solitude, the sun. From beyond the fence the faint sound of traffic came. Within, in dust and silence, the battered front ends were set in rows, headlights missing, wheels gone. There was rust everywhere, spiders spinning beneath the dash. To one side, like a fated Panzer unit, were lines of Volkswagens, squarebacks, sedans, most of them down on their rear axles, their noses raised like dying beasts. There were stickers on the windows from Texas, Georgia, *Turista* Mexico.

He had a small apartment, two rooms and a kitchen, neat and somewhat bare. There was a wooden table with books above it on a shelf, a hammock, a wicker couch. The sun came through the windows in the morning and poured on the empty floor. He had few friends. On weekends he slept late. There was never a newspaper, not even a magazine. He was recovering from something, an illness, a wound. He had no plans. Occasionally he talked of buying a boat and one night, unexpectedly, about France.

"You've been to France?"

"I used to live there," he said.

"I didn't know that. When was that?"

"Oh, a while ago," he said. That was all.

Sometimes she found him lying in the hammock late at night, barefoot, the television on, arms folded over his head as if to keep out the light.

She began preparing dinner. It was almost evening, and had started to rain. She appeared from time to time in the doorway of the kitchen, passing back and forth. She was lanky, all arms and legs. The room grew slowly darker, the doorway more and more bright. There was the sound of her mixing things, running water. The refrigerator door opened and closed. She came into the room with a piece of buttered bread and a can of beer. She sat down beside him. The wind was blowing now, the window spattered with rain.

"Are you hungry?"

"Not very."

"Why don't we wait then?" she said. She looked at her knees. Her hair was unfastened and hanging down. She gathered it idly in her hand. "I had a letter from Fraser," she said.

"Oh, yeah?"

"From Atlanta. He's quit drinking, he says. Even has a job." The gusts of rain were sweeping against the house. "He wants me to come back," she said.

There was a silence.

"I thought that was all finished."

She shrugged.

"Do you want to go?"

She didn't answer. After a moment he turned away. It was as if he'd forgotten her, as if he were thinking about something else. There were always long waits with him, like descents.

"Why are you telling me?" he said finally.

"Don't you want to know?"

He didn't say anything. It was too much trouble to explain. He didn't want to live again anything he had already lived. He did not want it all repeated.

"It's really raining. It looks like a storm," he said. The words, the sentences were jammed and awkward. He could not seem to work them free. "You want me to tell you what to do? Don't go back," he said.

"Why not?"

"It's finished. Once it's over, it's over."

"Not always," she said.

"Well, maybe you're right," he said. "I guess there are no rules."

"I really don't know what you want," she said. "That's the thing."

"I don't think that's the thing."

"I don't really know you."

"You say you don't, but you do. You know, all right. I'm a fake," he said calmly, "just like the rest of them."

There was silence. He sat there.

"You know, I'm thirty-four," she said.

"Is that right?"

"Yes."

"I thought you were thirty-two."

"No, I'm thirty-four. I just thought you should know."

"That's not so bad."

"I want to trust someone," she said. She was not looking at him but at the floor. "I want to feel something. With you, though, it's like somehow it goes into empty air."

"Empty air . . ."

"Yes."

"Well, what you have to do is hold on," he said. "Don't get scared."

"I am scared."

"Hold on."

"That's it?"

"I can't tell you any more than that. It wouldn't be the truth."

"Hold on . . . ," she said.

"That's right."

He sees it there in the darkness, not a vision, not a sign, but a genuine shelter if he can only reach it. In the lighted room are figures, he sees them clearly, sometimes seated together, sometimes moving, a man and a woman visible through the window, in the dusk, the Florida rain.